FEAR ITSELF

BENJAMIN PRATT & THE
KEEPERS OF THE SCHOOL

FEAR ITSELF

BOOK 2

ANDREW CLEMENTS

ILLUSTRATED BY ADAM STOWER

Atheneum Books for Young Readers
New York London Toronto Sydney

ATHENEUM BOOKS FOR YOUNG READERS
An imprint of Simon & Schuster Children's Publishing Division
1230 Avenue of the Americas, New York, New York 10020

This book is a work of fiction. Any references to historical events, real people, or real locales are used fictitiously. Other names, characters, places, and incidents are products of the author's imagination, and any resemblance to actual events or locales or persons, living or dead, is entirely coincidental.

For information about special discounts for bulk purchases, please contact Simon & Schuster Special Sales at 1-866-506-1949 or business@simonandschuster.com.
The Simon & Schuster Speakers Bureau can bring authors to your live event. For more information or to book an event, contact the Simon & Schuster Speakers Bureau at 1-866-248-3049 or visit our website at www.simonspeakers.com.
Book design by Sonia Chaghatzbanian
The text for this book is set in Veronan.
The illustrations for this book are rendered in pen and ink.
Manufactured in the United States of America
1210 FFG
First Edition
10 9 8 7 6 5 4 3 2 1
Library of Congress Cataloging-in-Publication Data
Clements, Andrew, 1949–
Fear itself / Andrew Clements ; illustrated by Adam Stower. — 1st ed.
p. cm. — (Benjamin Pratt and the Keepers of the School)
Summary: As the new Keepers of the School, sixth-graders Ben and Jill must decipher a handful of clues written as maritime riddles to save their school from demolition by a greedy company.
ISBN 978-1-4169-3887-3
[1. Mystery and detective stories. 2. Schools—Fiction. 3. Riddles—Fiction.] I. Stower, Adam, ill. II. Title.
PZ7.C59118Fe 2010
[Fic]—dc22   2010015876

For Bob and Meg Waterhouse
—A. C.

.

FEAR ITSELF

CHAPTER 1

Hero to Zero

Benjamin Pratt had some serious detective work to do, so his plan was to be invisible all day, to do nothing that would draw attention to himself. He was going to glide around the Captain Oakes School like a ghost, observing, examining, analyzing. He had a fresh pack of index cards for organizing his notes, and he'd brought his good digital camera, a tiny thing not much bigger than a pack of gum. He also had a small flashlight and a twelve-foot tape measure. Secret agent stuff.

But the invisibility wasn't happening, not today.

"Ben, way to go!"

"Hey, Pratt—saving Gerritt and everything? Amazing!"

Before he got to his homeroom on Monday he'd been high-fived four times, and had been called a hero, the champ, Mr. Lifeguard, and Aquaman.

True, he had in fact dived into the choppy ocean to help Robert Gerritt after the guy flipped his sailboat during their race on Saturday. But only because he'd been right there when it happened—what, was he supposed to just watch a kid drown?

When a crowd of reporters had gathered at his mom's house Saturday evening with lights and cameras, she had scolded them off her lawn. Ben didn't have anything more to say about it—another boy had been in trouble, and her son had helped out, that was all.

But Robert had had plenty to say.

Propped up in a hospital bed with a bandage wrapping his head, he had talked to everybody. The incident was called "Rescue at Sea" on one Boston TV station and "Escape from Death" on another—a colorful news story both Saturday and Sunday.

To Ben's surprise, Robert had actually given him some credit.

Looking straight into the camera, he'd said, "Yeah, if it hadn't been for Ben, I might not have made it."

2

RESCUE AT SEA

However, Robert had also said, "But the worst part? It happened just as I was about to win my first big sailing race of the year!"

Typical.

And today, with everyone treating Ben like a celebrity, he didn't see how he'd get to do much exploring. Which was too bad—he really needed some fresh ideas.

All weekend he had been chewing on the clues he and Jill had found on Friday, clues that were supposed to help them find stuff—stuff that would somehow keep their school from being torn down ... that would somehow keep the Glennley Entertainment Group from building their massive theme park on the harbor ... that would somehow keep the whole town of Edgeport from turning into a huge, neon tourist trap.

That was the mission, and it seemed impossible. Plus completely crazy.

After the final bell clanged for homeroom, everyone stood up and recited the Pledge of Allegiance, and then the principal began reading the announcements. But Ben couldn't think about anything except those clues. They ran through his mind for the hundredth time:

AFTER FIVE BELLS SOUND, TIME TO SIT DOWN.
AFTER FOUR TIMES FOUR, TREAD UP ONE MORE.
AFTER THREE HOOKS PASS, ONE WILL BE BRASS.
AFTER TWO TIDES SPIN, A MAN WALKS IN.
AFTER ONE STILL STAR, HORIZONS AFAR.

He had called Jill twice on Sunday and again this morning before school to ask if she'd made any progress.

"Give it a rest, Benjamin. I *know* we need a break-through—but, like, what are we looking for? And where are we supposed to start? And what could we possibly find that could actually stop these people? The Glennley Group has spent *thirty-five million dollars*. They *own* the school. And on June eighteenth, they're going to rip it down. I've got to eat breakfast. Good-bye."

She'd sounded angry, discouraged, too, which wasn't like her. Ben couldn't figure it out. Jill had been rock solid last Friday, and she'd seemed great when he'd seen her after the sailboat race on Saturday. So . . . something must have happened over the rest of the weekend. But what? He had no idea. Whatever was bothering her, it wasn't good. Because Ben was pretty sure that without Jill's help on this, they might as well go ahead and buy the cheap lifetime passes that Tall Ships Ahoy! had advertised in Sunday's *Boston Globe*.

But he'd see Jill in third-period math for sure, and maybe he'd have something figured out by then. Or at least have an idea about what to do next. Maybe she just needed to feel like they were making some real progress. Ben was ready to try anything to cheer her up a little.

Ms. Wilton took attendance, then laid out the week's schedule. When she finished, there were still about ten minutes before first period. So Ben got out a pencil and a blank index card and started thinking.

He thought about the copper plate he and Jill had found in a secret compartment on the third floor—a message hidden there by the first Keepers of the School back in 1791. One particular sentence about Captain Oakes in that message jumped out at him: *He prepared five safeguards to help us in our self-defense.*

Ben wrote the word "safeguards" on the card.

Maybe Jill was right. Maybe Captain Oakes was just a rich old weirdo who wanted lots of attention, the kind of guy who would stick his own grave in the middle of a school playground.

No, Ben was already sure there was something more to all this.

He thought about the message stamped on the gold coin Mr. Keane had given him, and then wrote two more words on the index card: "attack" and "defend."

Those were military terms.

Which made sense—after all, Captain Oakes was

a *captain*, a man of action, the guy in charge. He had commanded one of his own ships in the American navy during the Revolutionary War.

Ben stared at the three words he'd written and tried to imagine being a sea captain, being responsible for a large ship and the life of every person on it. The captain would have to oversee everything. His ship would sail thousands of miles, spend months at a time on the high seas. The captain would have to account for every barrel of water, every sack of flour, every yard of canvas, every musket and cannonball, every ounce of gunpowder, every length of rope.

So Captain Oakes wasn't some goofball. He must have been an amazing thinker, an incredible long-range planner.

And . . . as the captain was converting his warehouse into this school, it was like he was outfitting a ship for a trip—the long voyage into the future. And he was certain there would be dangers.

Ben remembered the old book the librarian had found for him, and what he'd read about the captain. Oakes had been very old by then, so he knew he wouldn't be around to command this new ship himself. If it ever came under attack, his officers would have to fight the enemy on their own. *But . . .* if he planned carefully and left the right kind of weapons—safeguards—then his ship and his crew would survive.

And who did the captain enlist as the commanders for his most important ship? The school janitors.

Ben smiled. That was pure genius, to choose steady, professional caretakers to defend his school, to carry that gold coin with their captain's instructions on it. And down through the years, each janitor had been responsible for finding his own replacement, someone trustworthy.

And the captain's plan had worked perfectly from 1783 right up to last Thursday. Except now, there wasn't a reliable janitor. Which was why Mr. Keane had given the coin to Ben.

So *I'm* the new commander, he thought, and his smile got bigger.

But it faded as he thought about Mr. Keane. Just hours after handing the coin to Ben, he had died. And he had warned Ben about his assistant janitor, Lyman: "He's a snake."

Worse than a snake, thought Ben.

He was a spy, working for the company that had

bought the school—after they'd figured out how to get around the captain's last will and testament.

Lyman was a big problem.

"Ben?"

He looked up to see his homeroom teacher holding out her hand, and he took a slip of paper from her.

"I almost forgot. Mrs. Sinclair wants to see you in the library before first period."

"Oh—okay."

He tucked the index card in his pocket and stood up.

"And Ben, I heard about what you did this weekend. I'm proud of you."

"Thanks," he said, beginning to blush, "but really, I was just the closest one to the accident."

"Well," Ms. Wilton said, "I'm proud of you anyway—we all are," and there were nods of agreement from the kids around him.

Ben smiled awkwardly, his face bright red now. He grabbed his book bag and rushed out the door.

So much for being invisible.

The library was on the opposite corner of the first floor, and as he walked through the quiet hallway, Ben knew why Mrs. Sinclair wanted to see him. He and Jill were doing a big social studies project, a report about the history of the Oakes School—which would give them extra time in the building to search for the stuff the captain had left behind, the safeguards.

A brilliant plan—*his* brilliant plan.

Except Robert Gerritt had butted his way into the project. So that would be a drag. And a complication—one more among a jillion others.

Ben shook his head. This whole thing was crazy. In less than a month the school was scheduled for demolition, and two kids were supposed to stop it all by themselves? But Ben caught himself, made himself stop thinking that way—he was sounding like Jill! And if they *both* got discouraged, that really would be the end. He had to keep fighting. Still . . . it all seemed pretty insane.

When he walked in from the hallway, Mrs. Sinclair saw him. She nodded toward the glass-walled workroom over in the center of the library. "I'll be with you in a minute, Ben."

The library was his favorite place in the old school, so he was glad to have a moment to just sit and look around. It was a large space, and the high ceiling made it feel open and airy. Dark oak bookshelves ran along all four walls of the main room. The shelf edges had been carved to look like thick rope, and the panels along the top of each unit had also been decorated. Some of the carvings showed scenes of ships at sea, complete with waves and clouds and flapping flags. There were carvings of small New England farms and busy seaports, and Ben's favorite showed a large deer standing on a wooded hillside. The designer of the room had added three shallow alcoves, which broke up the boxy feeling of the long shelves. Centered on the north, east, and west walls, each alcove had a dark oak table and comfy cushioned benches. Wide leaded-glass windows facing east and north let in lots of daylight. Even though the center area had been updated with modern tables and chairs and computer workstations, the original flavor of the room had survived. The place smelled like time.

Looking around, Ben's thoughts drifted again to Captain Oakes and the safeguards he and Jill had to find. He was glad the library was going to be sort of like the command center for their project, a place they could come before and after school. And since he and Jill would need to make lots of drawings and

take lots of photos for the report, they would be able to wander around the school pretty much wherever they wanted to. At least, that was the plan.

His brilliant plan.

Mrs. Sinclair came into the workroom and stood in front of him. He looked up with a smile—which disappeared when he saw her face.

"The book is missing, Ben, the one you used on Friday." Her voice was flat and cold. "I took it off the reference shelf for you, and you promised to be careful with it. But this morning, Ms. Shubert noticed it wasn't there."

Ben felt his throat tighten, felt his face start to get hot. "But I—"

She held up a hand. "No, let me finish. I haven't talked about this with Mr. Telmer, or with anyone else. I wanted to speak to you first. If for some reason you misunderstood me, and you took that book out of the library, then you can simply return it. And as long as it isn't damaged, that will be the end of this. All right?" She looked him in the eye. "Now, what do you have to say?"

CHAPTER 2

The Jaws
of Defeat

She thinks I'm a thief!

Ben sat there with his mouth open, a hundred different thoughts exploding in his head as the librarian waited for an explanation.

The missing book, the old one about how Captain Oakes founded the school? He had definitely looked at it on Friday. And taken photos of some drawings. And then he had definitely put it back on the shelf. He was sure of it.

He had *not* stolen that book. Period.

But . . . *someone* had been watching him. On Friday. In the library.

So he could just explain. . . . *Well, you see, Mrs. Sinclair, right before Mr. Keane died, he gave me this gold coin with some writing on it, and now* I'm *the person in charge of following Captain Oakes's orders to defend his school. And Mr. Lyman, the other janitor? Well, you see, he* actually *works for the company that's going to tear the school down and build the amusement park here. And Lyman knows* I *was the last person at school who talked to Mr. Keane, so he's been spying on me—in case I really do figure out a way to mess up the big plans. So I'm pretty sure that* Lyman's *the guy who stole that book.*

Right.

Tell *that* to Mrs. Sinclair, and she'd be calling the loony squad in three seconds flat. Every bit of it was true . . . but he was sworn to secrecy—right?

Still . . . what if telling her the complete truth, right now, what if *that* was the only way to keep himself out of trouble, keep things steady so he and Jill could go on with their searching? Because this situation could wreck everything. Wouldn't saving the school be more important than keeping the secret?

Maybe Mrs. Sinclair would believe him; maybe she'd even help look for the safeguards; maybe she'd . . .

15

Her eyes flashed. "Well? I'm waiting."

Ben had to say something.

He took a deep breath . . . and the assistant librarian, Ms. Shubert, hurried into the room.

"Mrs. Sinclair?"

The librarian turned, clearly annoyed with the interruption. "What?"

"Um . . ." The assistant came close and whispered in her ear.

As Mrs. Sinclair listened, Ben watched her expression change from irritation . . . to sheer horror. Her face went pale.

She looked back to Ben and spoke, almost in a whisper. "You—you'll have to excuse me a moment."

She rushed out of the workroom and went right to the front desk, followed by Ms. Shubert.

Ben craned his neck, but all he could see was the two of them, staring at a piece of paper. Then Mrs. Sinclair picked up a large brown envelope, looked inside, and set it down on the desk.

She said something to Ms. Shubert, then headed back toward him. Ben knew his time was up. He had to say something.

He decided to risk it. He had to tell her *every-thing*. Right now.

"Mrs. Sinclair, I—"

"No, please. Don't say a word." She paused, and took a deep breath. "Ben, I am so, *so* sorry. And embarrassed. The book, the one about the school? It's out there on the front desk. And there's a note from a staff member who borrowed it over the weekend. It's a valuable book, and when Ms. Shubert noticed it was gone this morning, I jumped to a very wrong conclusion. And I hope you'll forgive me—I feel *terrible* about this. I had a hard time imagining you would ever steal anything, Ben, really. This is just an awful mistake . . . *my* mistake."

The librarian looked miserable. Again, Ben didn't know what to say.

So he gave her a big smile. "It's okay, Mrs. Sinclair, really. I mean, I knew I hadn't done anything wrong. And actually"—he paused, thinking fast—"in homeroom, when I got your note, to come to the library? I thought you wanted to talk about the big history project I'm doing with Jill Acton. And Robert Gerritt. For social studies."

"A research project? How *exciting*!" She seemed

thrilled to have something else to talk about.

Ben felt like grinning, because this mess? It was actually perfect—the worse the librarian felt, the more she'd want to help them with their project.

Ben kept his face earnest and serious. "Well," he said, "we want to learn about the history of the school, especially since it's getting torn down and everything. And we asked Mrs. Hinman to talk to you because we need a place to come before school—and after school too. And maybe during lunch. That's why I was looking at that book, because of our project. And we wanted you to help us too. Didn't Mrs. Hinman talk to you?"

"No, no, she didn't, but I think this is a *grand* idea, and I'll make sure that the full resources of the media center are at your disposal. And I'll talk to Mrs. Hinman this morning when she comes in with her second-period class. Oh, this just sounds *wonderful*!"

"Great," said Ben. "Um . . . do you think you could make out hall passes for Jill and me . . . and also for Robert? Because we need to get started right away, like, today."

"Why, of course I can." She stepped to her desk, opened a drawer, and took out a pad of bright yellow forms. As she began writing, she said, "This is a wonderful idea, and it'll be exciting to see what you discover."

"Yeah," said Ben, "we're excited about it too."

Ben wasn't kidding when he said that, but the idea of telling Jill about everything that had just happened—*that* was going to be fantastic. He began building the story in his head—first he'd tell her how he'd stayed cool when Mrs. Sinclair had accused him, how he had forgiven her when she discovered her mistake, and then how he had used the situation perfectly to enlist her complete support. He, Benjamin Pratt, had just plucked a victory from the jaws of defeat! And the story he told Jill was going to be upbeat, positive, strong—and maybe he would come right out and ask her why she'd been so down about everything earlier, get her to open up a little, really get her back on board.

The ship's bell clanged for the end of homeroom, and as the librarian handed him the three passes, Ben stood up. "Well, thanks, Mrs. Sinclair. This'll really help us a lot."

"I'm glad, and thank you for understanding about the book, Ben. I'm *so* sorry about the mistake."

Ben shrugged and smiled. "Everything worked out fine. So, I'll see you later."

"Yes . . . and by the way, Ben, what you did on Saturday, saving Robert that way? That was quite something."

"Thanks . . . lots of other people helped too. But thanks."

Leaving the workroom, Ben didn't head straight for the door. He walked by the front desk, and as he passed, he glanced at the sheet of paper lying next to the large envelope.

The handwriting was small, but boxy and clear. Black ink.

Ben had no trouble reading the signature at the bottom of the note:

J. Lyman

He wasn't surprised—but it still sent a shiver through him, and as he left the library he took an anxious look down the hallway, first one way, then the other. He turned right and hurried toward the walkway into the Annex, barely aware of the kids around him, not aware of anything except this sudden feeling of vulnerability. Because this business with the old book? It was the clearest proof yet that Lyman *knew* Ben was up to something, that the man was actively following him, watching him.

As uncomfortable as that made him feel, something else scared him even more: Lyman had probably studied that book all weekend long, examining the carpenter's detailed drawings, thinking about each staircase, each beam, locating each bricked-up fireplace. He could have made a list of every possible hiding place in the whole school. Lyman was smart, and he was deadly serious—and now he was on high alert, ready to defend against anything that might stop the theme park. There was no telling what he might have discovered. Or what his next move might be.

By the time he had reached the long corridor at the east end of the Annex, all Ben's confidence, all his enthusiasm, all his courage to deal with the challenges ahead—all of it was gone, vanished. And at that moment he understood Jill's mood exactly. Because now *he* was the one feeling discouraged. And outsmarted. And under attack. And . . . scared.

NO!

Ben clenched his jaw and shoved the door aside as he walked into the chorus room.

He was *not* going to let *this* or anything else stop him. *He* was responsible for this ship now. Did Lyman and his bosses think he was going to get all shaky and go hide under his bunk? Well, they were wrong. If they wanted a fight, then he was ready— Benjamin Pratt, on deck and reporting for duty!

He dropped his book bag behind the risers and picked up his packet of music. He looked like he was just another kid getting ready to sing, but in his mind a battle was raging. And he was winning.

CHAPTER 3

No Such Thing

"What have you got so far?"

"Not much," said Jill, "but it's a start." She pulled out a sheet of paper and laid it on the table.

Ben and Jill had eaten lunch quickly, and then used their hall passes to get from the cafeteria to the library. Sitting in the alcove on the east wall of the large room, they still had fifteen minutes before the next period.

Of course, Robert was also there. The gauze and tape that had wrapped his head at the hospital had been replaced by a small bandage that covered the seven stitches above his left eye. He was working at a table over in the far corner, "'cause I don't want you losers stealing my ideas."

Ben looked at the neat columns of words and phrases on Jill's paper, amazed all over again at her talent for organization. Using the tip of her pencil, she began a guided tour, but she seemed halfhearted, almost casual about it, as if she were trying to stifle a yawn. It was a rotten attitude, but Ben didn't think it was the right moment to challenge her about it.

"Okay," she said, "the clue is, 'When five bells sound, time to sit down.' So first, what kind of a bell was Captain Oakes talking about? It could have been a church bell, a school bell, a ship's bell, a doorbell, a dinner bell, a clock chime, a fire bell, or maybe some other kind of warning bell. And here, when it says '*time* to sit down'? The five bells are the signal, and then comes the sitting down part."

Jill tapped her pencil at the top of the second column of words.

"Now, you have to sit down on *something*. So it makes sense that we're looking for a chair, or a bench, or a stool, or a school desk, or maybe a window seat, something like that, except it has to be something that's been here ever since the school was built."

"Yeah . . . ," Ben said slowly, "but actually, you can

sit on just about anything, like a railing or a step, a low wall, even a gravestone, right?"

"Well . . . yes," Jill said, "but I think the captain's carpenter was part of this hiding process—like with the way the copper plate was hidden up on the third floor, the fancy woodworking? So whatever we're looking for, I think it's going to be made of wood."

Ben shook his head. "We don't know for sure that the carpenter was involved . . . plus, a ship's carpenter had to be able to fix almost anything, and sometimes he would have to use copper or lead or canvas, even iron bars and plates—all sorts of materials. We shouldn't rule out anything."

Jill glared at him. "So is this the way it's going to be? I beat my brains out thinking up a bunch of new ideas, and then you sit there and tear them to bits?"

Ben stared at her, surprised. This went way beyond a bad attitude. "What are you talking about? It's not like I gave you orders to go 'beat your brains out' on this. After homeroom I told you what happened this morning in the library, and then *you're* the one who said you might have some time to think about it during second period, and how you wanted to crack the clue in a hurry. And now you're showing me your ideas, and I'm just thinking out loud. I mean, if *I* had pulled a bunch of stuff together, then *you'd* be the one reacting to it, right?"

Jill kept glaring at him.

Ben was tempted to glare right back and say, *Okay, what's really going on here? Why all the drama?* But he decided not to push it. Besides, maybe she was in a bad mood because of something simple . . . like not getting enough sleep over the weekend. Her face did look kind of pale today, and there were dark circles under her eyes. Maybe she just wasn't feeling well. Anyway, if something was really bothering her, she wasn't going to tell him anything until she was good and ready, no matter what. Better to back off a little.

"Look," he said, being careful with his tone of voice, "you're smarter than I am, and tons more organized. I know that. And I know how much I need your help with all this. But I also know that I still get a good idea now and then, you know, like one or two a month. And when I ask questions and stuff, I'm just trying to figure things out. It's not like I'm attacking you, or saying you're stupid. Stubborn, maybe"—he paused to grin—"but never stupid. Okay?"

She heaved a grumpy sigh, but Ben thought he saw a hint of a smile. "Okay," she said. "Anyway, that's all I've got. So . . . what now?"

Ben felt like he had his co-commander back on board, but just barely. It was time to take charge, to jump into action, to move things forward—which would be good for morale.

"Well . . . there's definitely a bell here at school, right? The one just inside the office door. And it sure looks like it's been there since the school began. So let's go take a look. And I'll take a picture of it. For our report."

Jill rolled her eyes. "Whoop-de-doo—we're going to take a picture of a bell. Sounds thrilling." But she put her papers into a folder and stood up. "Well, don't just sit there, Pratt. Let's go."

Back at his table Robert was hunched over a book, taking furious notes. He barely glanced up as they headed for the door.

Ms. Shubert was at the front desk, and Ben said, "Is it okay if we leave our stuff on the table in that alcove for a few minutes? We've got to go to the office."

She smiled. "No problem. I'll keep an eye on everything."

Ben stopped at the library entrance and peeked to the right and then the left before stepping into the hallway, and about five seconds later he looked over his shoulder. He noticed that he was tapping his tongue against the back of his two front teeth—a nervous habit.

"Relax," Jill said, trying to sound bored. "Lyman's the only janitor now, and there are three lunch periods in a row. He's stuck in the cafeteria with mop-up duty for at least an hour."

"See?" Ben grinned at her. "Figuring out stuff like that? *That's* why you are completely indispensable."

When they walked into the office, Mrs. Hendon was at her desk back behind the counter, a spoon in one hand and a container of yogurt in the other.

She looked up at them and smiled. "Hi, Jill. Hi, Ben. May I help you?"

Ben held up his hall pass. "We're working on a project about the history of the school, and we wanted to look at the old bell. Is that okay?"

"Sure," she said, nodding to the right of the door. "It's right there, but be careful not to ring it—it's very loud." She went back to her lunch.

Ben got out his camera. He had heard this bell

ring every school day since the beginning of fourth grade, but had never really looked at it. Hanging from an iron bracket, it was just above his eye level, and he stood on tiptoe to get a better look.

The bell hadn't been polished for at least a hundred years, was his first thought. The brass had turned a deep blackish brown. But there was lettering on it, engraved, cut deeply enough into the metal that he could still read it. He nudged Jill and whispered, "Check out the name of the ship this came from— HMS *Safeguard*!"

She shrugged, as if she wasn't interested.

But Ben was genuinely excited, and he snapped three photos.

Two bronze plaques were attached to the wall, one on either side of the bell. The metal edges seemed like they were buried in the wall, but Ben saw it was just from all the coats of paint that had built up over the years.

The plaque to the right of the bell was a history lesson.

On December 16, 1778, HMS *Safeguard* entered Barclay Bay under cover of darkness and directed cannon fire at the town of Edgeport. USS *Stalwart*, commanded by Captain Duncan Oakes, engaged the enemy. After a heated exchange, the British ship caught fire and burned to the waterline, and her officers and crew were taken captive. Timber salvaged from the *Safeguard* was later used to make the library shelves, classroom doors, student desks, and many other fixtures in this school.

"Cool!" Ben whispered, and he took two photos of the plaque, one straight on, and the other from an angle that also got the bell in the frame.

Keeping the camera up in front of his face, he switched his aim and snapped a couple of quick pictures of the plaque to the left of the bell.

Then he looked at the inscription—and almost dropped his camera.

"Hey!" Ben whispered. "Check this out!"

Jill was sitting on the bench to the left of the office door, looking at last week's school newsletter. Ben was getting sick and tired of her "I'm so bored" act, but he was too excited to lose his temper.

She came and stood beside him, then squinted at the plaque.

        ONE BELL •
        TWO BELLS ••
        THREE BELLS •• •
        FOUR BELLS •• ••
        FIVE BELLS •• •• •
        SIX BELLS •• •• ••
        SEVEN BELLS •• •• •• •
        EIGHT BELLS •• •• •• ••

"What's that?" she said. "Morse Code or something?"

Ben shook his head. "I should have thought of

this—my dad gave me a book, and there's this story, 'Death at Eight Bells,' about a sailor who's going to be hung from the yardarm at the end of the morning watch. Those dots? They show how to ring the bell in different patterns. It was how they used to keep time on board a ship. When the bell rang a pattern, everyone could tell what time it was. And one group of sailors got up and went on duty, and the group that had been standing watch got to rest." He ran a finger across the five raised dots. "See? Five bells! 'When five bells sound, time to sit down'!"

Jill nodded, "It's interesting, but . . ."

"But what?"

"Well," she said, "it doesn't really help us *find* anything, does it? I mean, *this* bell never rings the pattern for five bells. It's always one clang for an announcement, or three at the beginning and end of a period. And that's actually just a recording of the bell, played through speakers."

Ben frowned at the plaque. "I still think it's important. I mean, this bell is from the *Safeguard*!"

Jill shrugged. "That could just be a coincidence."

"A coincidence? Maybe . . . ," Ben said, "but I'm starting to feel like there's no such thing."

Jill turned away, then nudged his arm. "Look!" she whispered.

It was Lyman, walking straight for the office.

"Like I said," muttered Ben, "no such thing."

CHAPTER 4

Eye of the Tiger

Lyman came into the office and walked directly to the counter without even glancing at Ben or Jill.

Mrs. Hendon looked up. "Hi, Jerry. What can I do for you?"

"Hi, Rita. I was expecting a letter from the payroll office, and I think it landed in somebody else's mailbox. I didn't want to go poking around myself—could you take a quick look?"

"Sure thing," she said, putting down her yogurt and heading for the wide rack of wooden cubbyholes.

Jill had already walked out into the hallway. Ben felt his heart thumping, felt his mouth getting dry, and his instinct was to get out of there fast. He almost bolted.

But then he remembered the way he'd felt earlier, at the beginning of chorus. And he asked himself the same question.

Was he going to get all shaky and go hide under his bunk?

Ben jammed a big smile onto his face and forced himself to sound loud and cheerful. "Hey, this is great—perfect timing! Mrs. Hendon, would you mind if I took a picture of you with Mr. Lyman? We want to get photos of all the staff as part of our school history project. And you two? You're the ones who really make the school *work*."

Mrs. Hendon smiled and touched her hair. "That's a sweet idea, Ben, but I don't think . . ."

"Please?" said Ben. "It'll just take a second."

"Oh, all right," she said, still adjusting her hair. She quickly stepped around the counter and stood next to Lyman.

"Okay," Ben said, "smile . . . one, two—come on, Mr. Lyman, a really *big* smile . . . perfect . . . and . . . three!" The camera flashed. "Great! And I'll be sure you both get a copy. Thanks!"

As he stepped out into the hall, Ben heard Mrs. Hendon say, "He is such a *nice* young man!" He didn't hear Lyman's reply.

Ben felt like he was floating above the floor as he and Jill hurried toward the library.

When they rounded the corner in the hallway, Jill said, "What was all that about?"

"*That*," said Ben, "was a victory. And it was about letting Lyman know I'm not afraid of him."

"Well, if you ask me," said Jill, "it was stupid. You *should* be afraid of him. The less contact either of us has with that man, the better."

Ben shook his head. "You said it yourself: With Mr. Keane gone, he's focused on me now, and on you, too. And we have to deal with it. This is a big building, and he can't be everywhere at once. We can keep ahead of him—*and* we know things he doesn't."

"Correction," said Jill. "We have some *clues*—we don't actually *know* anything."

"Well, not yet," Ben admitted.

Jill nodded. "Exactly. And until you're sure there's a cage around a tiger, it's pretty dumb to dangle meat in front of it. Right?"

Ben was feeling clever, and he wasn't going to let

Jill get the last word. "Yes . . . but sometimes you have to look it in the eye and let it know you're not scared. And that's what I just did. I looked a tiger in the eye . . . and then I said, 'Smile!' And I'm *glad* I did it."

Jill shook her head. "I still say it was stupid."

Robert was just leaving as they walked back into the library. "Hi—found some great stories about the school, amazing pictures, too."

"Yeah?" said Ben. "Like what?"

"You'll hear about it—when I give *my* part of the report. Catch you later." He turned toward the Annex, then stopped and said, "Hey, did that guy find you?"

Ben stiffened. "What guy?" But he already knew.

"The janitor. He was in here cleaning up over where you were working. He asked if I knew where you were, thought you might have left your things here by mistake."

"Yeah," Ben said, "he found us. Thanks."

"No problem."

Jill was already at the table in the alcove, opening her backpack. "Was there anything in your bag," she asked, "anything he could have taken?"

"Nope," he said, patting his pockets. "Got it all

right here. How about your backpack? Anything missing?"

"No, I took my folder with me.
But my books are all out of order—someone went
through them."

Jill's eyes suddenly got huge. She grabbed Ben's
arm, put a finger to her lips, and shook her head.

He got the message instantly—bugs! Lyman
could have planted a listening device in the alcove—
or even in their backpacks! Ben was jolted by that
same sick feeling he'd gotten after Lyman's visit to
the sailboat—only this seemed like more of a direct
attack. If the man was listening, it was time to give
him an earful.

Nodding at Jill, Ben said, "You know, I don't think
it's legal to look through someone's book bag. You
know my dad's brother, the one on the Beverly police
force? I'm gonna call him and ask about this."

Jill made a face at him. No way did he have an
uncle who was a cop.

Ben felt like he had to keep trying to sound
natural. "Anyway, we'd better get to fourth period.
You want to hang out after school?"

"Can't, I've got orchestra."

Ben was pretty sure that was true. "Well, I could come work in here after school. How long's your rehearsal?"

"Only a half hour today."

"Good—so maybe we can walk down to the harbor after, okay?"

"Sure," she said.

Out in the hallway Jill was furious, walking so fast Ben almost had to trot to keep up. "What did I tell you?" she hissed. "Lyman is a *professional*, and I am *not*, and neither are you."

"Well, you're the one who said, 'Oh, relax, Ben, he's stuck in the cafeteria.'"

"Yes," Jill said, nodding, "and I was wrong. We have to remember that Lyman is *not* the school janitor. He's an undercover agent *pretending* he's a janitor."

They went through the doors into the long hallway that led to the Annex.

"And," Jill went on, "he's got a huge budget to work with, and he probably has all the latest spy equipment. He could have planted GPS tracking devices in our backpacks. He could be listening to us right now."

Ben shook his head. "He *could* be, but I bet he's

not. Hidden cameras and secret listening equipment and tracking bugs? Those things are totally illegal, especially if someone tried to spy on kids. And inside a public school? No way. People go to jail for stuff like that. No matter how much he's getting paid, I don't think Lyman would take that risk. I mean, *I* wouldn't—would you?"

"Of course not," said Jill, coming to a stop. "But *we're* not him. I'm just saying we have to be a *lot* more careful. And if we want to do something or go somewhere without him knowing about it, then we've got to have a strategy—like splitting up so one of us can be the lookout."

The bell clanged three times, and the hallway around them filled up with kids.

"I agree one hundred percent," said Ben. "Well, look, I've got to get up to the third floor. But we can't let this get us down, okay? 'Cause that stuff in the office about the bell? I'm almost sure it means something. We can figure this out. We just have to stay focused. Okay?"

Jill took a deep breath and let it out slowly. "All right," she said, "but you have to promise me something."

"What?" he asked.

"That you *won't* tease the tigers. Okay?"

Ben smiled and put his hand over his heart. "I promise. No more tiger teasing—at least not today."

"I'm serious, Benjamin."

"I know, I know—sorry. We are going to be super serious and super careful from now on. I'll text you tonight. You're headed to chorus, right?"

"Right," she said. "And you've got science now."

"Yeah."

"Well," she said lightly, "have fun with the quiz."

Ben stared at her. "There's a quiz? And you didn't tell me?"

Jill grinned. "Don't be scared—just look it in the eye and say, 'Smile.'"

CHAPTER 5

Odd, Odder, Oddest

Ben slipped into a pew at the back of the Seagate Chapel. Fifty or sixty people were standing up, singing a hymn. He felt embarrassed to be late for the service, but it had started at three, and he'd had to walk more than a mile from school.

Looking around a little, he spotted Mr. Telmer, the principal. Also a handful of teachers from Oakes School. It was weird to be the only kid in sight. Plus, he was the only person carrying a backpack, and the only person who wasn't dressed up. But there was no way he could have carried a coat and tie out of the house on a Monday morning without getting a million questions from his mom—questions he didn't want to

answer. It would have been tough to explain why he felt like he had to attend the funeral of the school janitor. But he did—he felt like he owed it to Mr. Keane.

This was only his second funeral ever. When his mom's father had passed away, he'd been four years old. All he remembered was his mom sniffling a lot and squeezing his hand so hard it hurt.

The hymn ended, and everyone remained standing. Up front, a woman wearing a long purple robe stood next to an easel that held a large framed photograph of Mr. Keane. She raised both palms, closed her eyes, and bowed her head.

"And now, let us go forward into our lives, confident that our friend Roger is safe, confident that the love of God is more powerful than sadness, more powerful than death itself. Amen."

The congregation murmured "Amen," and as the organ began playing again, everyone sat down while the minister led a small group of people up the aisle toward the back of the chapel.

Ben had a clear view. The little woman in the black dress had to be Mr. Keane's wife. And the stocky man at her elbow was definitely his son—same wild hair and bushy eyebrows.

Ben left the chapel and followed the others across Union Street and into the fellowship hall. Long tables were covered with all sorts of food—cheese and crackers, cookies and brownies, cakes, pies, several fruit platters, and eight or ten steaming casseroles.

Suddenly he was starving, and almost made a dash for the plates and forks. But just in time he realized there was a line, and he was in it. People were supposed to greet the grieving family before they stuffed their faces.

Fortunately, he was near the head of the line. About three minutes later he shook Mrs. Keane's hand and said, "I'm sorry for your loss. I'm Ben Pratt, from Oakes School. I . . . I knew your husband."

The woman wasn't much taller than Ben, and her eyes were as sharp and blue as her husband's. She held on to his hand as she leaned forward. "I'm glad you came," she said, and then whispered, "Roger told me about you, right at the end. Could you stop by our house next week, some day after school?"

He nodded and smiled a little, and then quickly moved to the right as the large woman behind him swooped in to hug the widow.

Mr. Keane's son was next in the receiving line.

Ben held out his hand and looked up into his face. The resemblance to his dad was startling. The son's handshake was quick and businesslike.

"Thanks for comin'."

The room was filling up quickly, and Ben had to work his way slowly toward the refreshments. He glanced to his right—and there was Lyman bobbing through the crowd, a head taller than almost everyone else. He sidestepped the reception line and took up a position by the wall, then just stood there, looking around.

Ben wanted to duck down low and head for an exit. But he stopped himself. After all, he belonged here, and Lyman didn't. Why should he let that guy make him feel scared? It took an effort, but Ben clamped his jaw tightly and turned his back on Lyman, and in less than a minute he'd reached the food tables.

He took a plate, and as he began loading it with chunks of cheese and tiny sandwiches, Ben realized that Mrs. Keane's whispered invitation hadn't surprised him. It even made sense, in an odd sort of way. In fact, over the past five days, all sorts of odd things had begun to seem normal, almost expected.

Like Lyman, for instance, standing way over there in the corner of the room now, sipping coffee from a Styrofoam cup. Yes, it was odd to see him there, slowly scanning the room with his dark, unsmiling eyes. But it would have seemed odder if he *hadn't* been there. Ben smiled as he took a big bite of chocolate cake—maybe he should go over and snap another picture of the guy.

No, he'd promised Jill he would keep a safe distance from the tigers.

He wished she had come . . . so he'd have someone to talk to. When they were in social studies together during fifth period, he had almost invited her. Twice. *Hey, want to go to a funeral with me?* But that had seemed *really* odd. So he'd chickened out. Twice.

Anyway, Jill had orchestra practice. And with that sour attitude of hers, maybe a funeral would have pushed her over the edge.

Still, he wished she had come. If they spent some time together, maybe she'd open up a little, tell him what was bugging her. Because *something* was definitely bugging her.

The fruit from one particular tray was especially

sweet, so Ben headed back for more. The man ahead of him had one hand on his aluminum walker while he filled his plate with the other, carefully picking out only strawberries and blueberries.

He glanced at Ben and handed him the big spoon. "Here you go, junior. Great-looking fruit, huh?"

Ben smiled and took the spoon. "Yeah, it's really good."

It was clear that the man wouldn't be able to use his walker and also carry his plate, so Ben said, "Can I help you with that?"

"Thanks. I'm headed for the nearest chair." He shuffled off to the right while Ben served himself.

He followed the man to a tiny round table, then waited while he wrestled himself into a chair. Ben sat down and slid the plate of fruit across to him.

The man grabbed his fork and dug in right away, then smacked his lips.

"Mmm, mmm—ripe berries in May! Too bad people have to die before you get fruit this good."

Ben looked around quickly, shocked to hear him talk like that.

He saw Ben's face and cocked an eyebrow at him. "Oops—I said that out loud, didn't I?"

Ben nodded.

He grinned. "Happens more and more. Can't tell you how many people I've upset just in the past three days. And the last funeral I went to? People were having so much fun I forgot and thought I was at a wedding. They threw me out for trying to dance with the widow."

Ben didn't know if he should smile or be more shocked. So he took a bite of melon and looked away— only to see Mrs. Keane walking straight toward their table. She came over and put a hand on the old man's shoulder, then bent down to kiss him on the cheek.

"I'm so glad you're here, Tom."

"Wouldn't have missed it, Maggie. Really sorry."

She smiled at Ben. "I was going to introduce you two, but I see this rascal already found you."

The man pointed at Ben. "Him? He's my new fruit carrier." Then he winked and said, "I was just telling him I might ask you for a dance in a minute, see if we can't cheer this party up a little."

Ben's mouth dropped open, but Mrs. Keane laughed.

She looked at Ben and said, "Don't believe a thing this man says, you hear me? He's the biggest liar in all of Massachusetts, and that's saying something."

She shook her finger at her friend and gave him another kiss on the cheek. Then she moved on to the next table.

The man dug into his fruit again, and Ben said, "She seems really nice."

"Tough as nails. She and Roger lost a baby daughter. No laughing at that funeral. But she bounced back from it . . . amazing. Tough as nails."

"So you've known them a long time?"

He wiped some strawberry juice off his chin with a napkin. "Yup, going on fifty years. Gave Roger his first job when he was a kid right out of the navy. Good people, both of them."

"Mr. Keane worked for you?"

"Not really. I took disability retirement when I was forty-five, hired Roger to take over for me. I was the custodian at Oakes School."

Ben almost choked on a grape. Coughing, he reached for some water and took three quick gulps before he realized it wasn't even his glass.

"You were the janitor there?"

"Sure was. Best job I ever had."

Ben tried to look casual, which was hard. He

glanced over his shoulder and saw Lyman was still in the far corner, talking now with a woman who was about half his height.

Turning back to the old man, he said, "I was with Mr. Keane at school, the morning of the day he died. And he mentioned your name to me. You're Mr. Benton, right?"

"Yup, but everybody calls me Tom."

Ben reached into his pocket. Then he put both hands on the table, cupped together. He opened them just enough for the man to see what he had. "He gave me this, that morning."

Tom stared a second, then pulled in a sharp breath. His eyes got wide, then narrowed as he looked up into Ben's face. "You? *You're* the new janitor?"

Ben smiled and shook his head. "No. Don't stare, but over my left shoulder, way in the corner, that tall guy? He's the janitor now, but Mr. Keane didn't trust him. So he gave this to me, and told me I had to try to keep the school from being torn down. So that's what I'm doing."

Ben put the coin back in his pocket.

Tom Benton's eyes were still narrowed. "And how's that going?"

"Not bad, I guess. I mean, we're just getting started—looking for things."

His eyes got wide again. "*We?* Who's we?"

"Just me and a friend of mine. Really smart. I needed help."

"Hmm. . . ." He paused, thinking about that. "What have you found so far?"

"A list of clues."

Tom nodded. "Good. I found that too—'on the upper deck.' There with the big key."

It was Ben wide-eyed now, and breathless. "The other things, the safeguards? Did you find them, too?"

Tom shook his head. "Didn't look. No reason to. Haven't thought about those clues for a long time. But I sure did back then. I knew that school like the back of my hand." His eyes seemed to film over. "A lot of history at that place . . . a lot of history."

He stuck his fork into a strawberry that was bigger than a golf ball and bit off half of it.

Ben said, "The first clue? It's about bells, and today—"

Tom stopped chewing. "'After five bells sound, time to sit down,'—right?"

"Exactly!" Ben said. This guy had an amazing

memory! "So today we looked at the ship's bell in the office. Do you think there's a link between the name on the ship's bell, the *Safeguard*, and the things we're looking for? Because they're called 'safeguards' . . . on the message from the Keepers."

Tom ate the other half of the strawberry, chewed and chewed, then swallowed. "Seems to me at one time, I *did* think that made sense. And I recall making a list of ideas. . . . It was a long time ago." He shrugged. "Well, my memory's not perfect, but everything's still there. Sort of like a shortwave radio station— clear some days, not so great on others. But I'll do some thinking, see if I come up with something. I still walk those halls almost every night, especially when I can't get to sleep. I see myself walking up the granite steps, in the front door, left past the office, and then straight into the south stairwell. The seventh step from the ground floor has a bad squeak, but only if you're carrying a bucket of water—it's the extra weight. You probably didn't know that."

Again, the filmy eyes.

Ben's cell phone vibrated in his pocket. He hadn't told his mom he'd be late getting home. He let the phone ring and kept his focus on Mr. Benton's face,

hoping he'd keep talking, and maybe remember something useful.

Mr. Benton was more interested in fruit. He
chased the last blueberry around the edge of his
plate, stabbed it, then plucked it off the fork.

"You know," he said, glancing briefly into Ben's
face again, "I think my old fishing tackle box might
still be in the workroom over at the school. Maybe
under the bench? I don't know. . . . I went looking for it
in my storage locker at the place I was staying about
a year ago? Couldn't find it. Used to take it to school
when I worked Saturdays. Sat out on the seawall and
cast for snappers about sundown. Caught some nice
ones too, if the day was warm enough."

He was quiet, tapping his fork on his plate, a smile
on his face. Then he looked back at Ben. "Be nice to get
that tackle box, 'specially if they really tear the place
down. Thought of it about a month ago and meant to
ask Roger to fetch it for me. Never made the call—
forgot all about it. And then he died. Funny what a
man remembers." Jerking his head toward Lyman over
in the corner, he said, "'Course, I could ask that fella,
though, couldn't I? Shouldn't be hard to—"

"Um," Ben said quickly, "Roger—I mean, Mr.

Keane? He told me to steer clear of that guy."
Actually, Ben didn't want Lyman anywhere near
Tom Benton. He might remember something, might
let something slip out.

Mr. Benton looked disappointed.

Ben said, "I mean . . . I could probably find your
tackle box. In the janitor's workroom, right? I could at
least see if it's there. What's it look like?"

"Well, let me see . . . ," he said, speaking slowly.
"It's all metal, and it's pale green, except for the rusty
spots. 'Bout as big as a loaf of bread. And it's kind
of heavy—lots of big lead sinkers for deepwater
fishing. Used to go out for haddock every few
weeks, went with my uncle James. In fact, he's the
one who gave me that tackle box back when I was
fifteen. . . . 'Course, James is gone now, died quite a
while ago. . . . Still, it'd be nice to have that box. Just
to have it . . . you know what I mean?"

"Yeah, I know what you mean," said Ben. "I'll see
what I can do."

"Thanks." Then Tom got a sheepish look on his
face. "Suppose I can ask a favor, another one?"

"Sure," Ben said.

"Could this stay just between us? I don't want

everyone thinking I'm this old geezer who's gone soft in the head about junk from his boyhood. I guess that's pride. . . ." And then he grinned. "As if folks don't already know I'm crazy!"

Ben kept a straight face. "I won't tell anyone—promise."

"Well . . . thanks."

Ben leaned across the table and put out his hand, and the man shook it.

"I'm really glad I got to meet you, Mr. Benton."

"Good to meet you, too. And call me Tom, okay?"

"Right. I've got to get home now, but if you remember something about the clues, or about the building, or maybe something about Captain Oakes, anything would be a huge help. It'd be great to talk again. And I want my friend to meet you."

He nodded. "You bet. Throw enough questions at me, something might bounce back at you. I'm at BayHaven Care, up on High Street. Got a view of the water. Not like the view from the school, but it's not bad. Come and see me anytime—I'm always there . . . unless I'm at a funeral with good food."

Ben stood up. "I will. And in the meantime, wish me luck."

Tom frowned. "Can't do that. 'Shallow men believe in luck. Strong men believe in cause and effect.' Ralph Waldo Emerson. My sixth-grade teacher had it up on the classroom wall."

"I'll remember that. Well, good-bye."

"So long."

Ben turned to go, and Tom said, "Wait a second."

"Yes?"

"You didn't tell me your name, son."

"Oh, sorry. I'm Ben, Benjamin Pratt."

"Benjamin. Good. You know . . . there is one thing I just remembered."

Ben leaned forward. "Yes?"

"I'm out of strawberries. Want to get me a refill?"

Ben smiled and picked up his plate. "Happy to."

Five minutes later he had said his good-byes to Mrs. Keane and her son and was out front on Union Street. He had his phone in his hand, thinking about what he was going to say to his mom.

"Young man?"

One of the servers from the hall was coming down the steps toward him, her white apron flapping in the sea breeze.

She bustled over and handed him a white bakery

bag. "Mrs. Keane asked me to give you this. She said there was going to be a lot of fruit and desserts left over, and she knew you'd enjoy some more."

Ben smiled as he pulled the bag open to look—a big piece of chocolate cake right on top. "This is great! Tell her thanks for me."

"I certainly will. Good-bye now."

He slipped the bag into his backpack and opened his phone again.

He was dreading this call. He had to explain to his mom why he was late . . . without actually telling her where he'd been . . . and without lying. Because if he told her he'd gone to Mr. Keane's funeral, she'd ask a million questions. Without Dad around, it seemed like she was on his case more than ever.

However . . . she had met the janitor when he'd helped Ben and his dad scrape the hull of the sailboat two summers ago. And he could just tell her that when he'd heard that his funeral was today, he'd felt like he should go and pay his respects. Because that was the truth.

And even if his mom thought that was odd—well, so what? Ben was pretty sure he actually *was* a little odd, but in a good way. His mom needed to start getting used to that, and the sooner, the better.

Yes. He'd tell her the truth and then deal with whatever came next.

He pushed the CALL button on his phone and hoped for the best.

CHAPTER 6

Multitasking

"I am not asking you, Ben, I'm *telling* you: If you're going to be late coming home from school, call me. Every single time—no exceptions, no excuses, no discussion. Got it?"

Ben nodded.

She slapped a big spoonful of mashed potatoes onto his plate. "I need to hear you say, 'Yes, Mom, I understand.'"

"Yes, Mom, I understand."

"All right then. Please pass the peas."

Sheesh. Ben couldn't remember the last time he'd seen his mom this mad. Even the dog was scared. Nelson huddled under the table, and Ben wished he could crawl down there with him. At times like these, a corgi was much better company than a mom.

He'd called her after the funeral and told her where he'd been. She hadn't sounded that upset over the phone, mostly relieved. Then when he'd arrived home around four thirty, she hadn't seemed mad at all. Even seemed sort of pleased that he'd done something thoughtful and considerate. That was an hour ago.

So something else must have happened since then. Something that upset her. But there was no point in asking what. Could have been anything. These days, it didn't seem to take much.

Ben felt a quick flash of anger at his dad for not being at the dinner table, for not being there to say, *Hey, sweetheart, take it easy—he's just a kid, and kids mess up. No big deal.* That's what he always used to say. At times like this.

Then he thought of his dad, sitting alone at the small table aboard their sailboat. The anger vanished.

Ben wasn't really hungry, not after all that food at the funeral. But he cut off a piece of meat, put it in his mouth, and said, "Mmm—great steak."

"Don't talk with food in your mouth. But thank you. I used that special seasoning you like."

Ben ate the rest of his meal quickly. This didn't seem like a good time to have a conversation. His mom must have felt the same way. She didn't talk much either, just a quick question about how Robert was doing, and a comment or two about her work at the realty office.

It was one of those comments that made Ben decide to risk a question. "You said home prices in Edgeport are falling, but prices for apartments and office buildings are going up? That doesn't make sense."

His mom smiled. "It only makes sense if you think about that new theme park. People don't want to *live* near a big tourist attraction, but they *do* want to have stores and hotels and restaurants near it. The last six months have been crazy, and once they start construction, I'm going to make a lot of sales—a *lot*!"

Ben gulped. "So . . . you're *happy* about the theme park?"

"Well," she said, "I wouldn't say I'm thrilled about it, and I know it's going to change the town. But it *is* happening, and I *am* a realtor, so I'd be pretty silly if

I didn't take advantage of it, wouldn't I? I mean, you'll be going to college in a few short years, and all that money has to come from somewhere. The timing's actually just about right."

Ben couldn't believe it—his own mom was happy about a bunch of plastic ships. And neon lights. And huge parking lots with swarms of tourists.

He cleared the table in silence.

Talking about making money had definitely cheered up his mom. As they finished cleaning up the kitchen, out of the blue she said, "Say, guess what I found on sale at the grocery store? *The Sea Hawk* with Errol Flynn—it's out on DVD."

"No way! *The Sea Hawk*? Awesome!" And Ben wasn't acting—it was a great adventure movie, one of his favorites. The scene where the hero escaped from the Spanish slave galley flashed through his mind—fantastic!

His mom was beaming. "So how about we watch it after your work's done?"

"Absolutely!" But then he groaned. "Problem is, I've got

a ton of homework, plus that extra credit work for social studies."

"Oh. And that's the project you're working on with Jill?"

He nodded. "Yeah, there's *so* much research."

"What kind of research?" she asked.

Ben wasn't sure if his mom really wanted to know, or if she was just talking to hide her disappointment about not watching the movie together.

"You know," he said, "reading in the library, searching online, studying the building itself, stuff like that."

"The building itself? You mean what it looks like, the architecture?"

"Kind of. But we're also trying to figure out the history of the construction. Because the place started out as a huge shipping warehouse, and they had to turn it into a school. And the carpenter who did most of the work, this man named John Vining? His tools are still there, right in the school. And his drawings, too. I love stuff like that."

"What did you say his name was—the carpenter?"

"John Vining."

"Hmm," she said. "I feel like I've heard that name somewhere."

"Really?" said Ben. "I thought that too. But I haven't made any connections yet."

"Well, maybe I'll remember. And it's fine about the movie—I have work I should be doing too."

"So . . . how about we watch it Friday?" said Ben.

She brightened up again. "That'll be perfect—a night at the movies. Popcorn and grape soda, some chocolate, the whole package." She gave him a quick hug, then kissed the top of his head. "Go do your homework."

As Ben swung his book bag onto his shoulder and headed for his room, he recalled what Tom Benton had said about the squeaky step in the south stairwell at school—the seventh one from the ground floor. He smiled. He liked counting footsteps too, always had, ever since he'd learned his numbers.

And going to his room, it was ten steps straight up the front stairs to the second floor, a left turn, eight paces along the hallway, and then another left into a doorway. Up four steps, a half turn to the right, and then six more steps to the landing. A quick turn to the left, push the door, and there it was—an attic

room so small that it made his cabin on the *Tempus Fugit* seem almost spacious. Everything was small—the bed, the single window between the exposed beams, the pine dresser, his desk. Even the doorway was small, and it only had part of a door. The corner above the doorknob had been cut off at an angle so it wouldn't scrape the slanted ceiling.

He tossed his bag onto the bed, then got his phone out. Jill was on speed dial, and in two seconds she said, "Hello?"

"Hey," he said. "How's it going?"

"Okay."

She sounded down, so Ben kept talking. "Guess what my mom said at dinner—she's actually *glad* about the new theme park, says it's going to be great for her real estate sales. Can you believe that?"

"Yes, I can," said Jill. "My dad's the same way—can't wait for the whole thing to take off."

Ben thought a second. "But your mom's been fighting the project from the start, right? How does *that* work?"

"They deal with it." Jill changed the subject. "So, I looked for you after orchestra. Guess you decided not to stay and study in the library."

"What?"

"You said you might stay after. At lunchtime."

"Oh, right," said Ben, "that. I was just kind of talking, you know . . . when we thought Lyman might have bugged that alcove? I had plans to go to Mr. Keane's funeral after school. It started at three."

"You had plans? How come you didn't ask me to go?"

"You said you had orchestra—and . . . I mean, it would have been great if you could have come. I was the only kid there. I almost asked you during social studies . . . twice."

"But you didn't," she said coldly. Then in a milder tone, "But I don't blame you. I wasn't exactly Little Miss Sunshine today, was I?"

"Well . . . no," Ben said carefully.

He wanted to ask her about that, but immediately she said, "So, what was it like?"

"The funeral? Well, I actually missed most of the service, but at the reception I met Tom Benton—he was the school janitor before Mr. Keane. And when I showed him the gold coin, you should have seen his face! He thought *I* was the new janitor. Lyman was there too, and I told Tom how Mr. Keane said not to trust him. I told him about you, too—how I told you the secret because I needed help with everything. And get this—he solved the directions on the coin, like, fifty years ago, actually found the copper plate and the big key, and then put them back! Isn't that great?"

"Did he hunt for anything else?" Jill asked.

"I asked him that same question. He said no, because there wasn't any reason to. But he said he thought about all the clues, and he might have come up with some good ideas . . . except he can't remember now because it was so long ago. But he said he'd keep thinking. I told him I wanted him to meet you."

Ben heard his mom's footsteps on the second floor, heard her open the hallway door to the attic. "Ben?" she called up the stairs. "I can hear you talking—time to hang up and get on your homework now."

He held his phone against his chest, "Okay. Just another minute—I'm talking to Jill . . . about our project."

"One minute, Benjamin."

"All right"—then into the phone, "Sorry, that was my mom. I've got a ton of homework."

Jill said, "Yeah, me too."

She sounded distant again. Maybe he really should have asked her to come this afternoon. Wasn't much he could do about it now. Got to keep moving forward.

"Listen," he said, "if you get a little time later tonight, could you maybe look online and see if there's anything about John Vining? We need to know more about that guy. And try to keep thinking about that first safeguard clue."

"Okay," she said with a sigh, "but I've got to tell you, it all feels pretty pointless."

"But it's not," Ben said. "If what we're doing is so pointless, then how come Lyman keeps dogging us around?"

"I don't know—maybe he's just a creep."

Ben almost snapped back with a reply . . . but arguing wasn't going to help.

"Well, anyway," he said, "I've got to get busy. But text me if you come up with anything, okay?"

"Okay. Bye."

"G'bye."

Ben sat and stared at his phone. Jill's moodiness was getting to him. Was she right? Was it all pointless? He had to admit that feeling so responsible for everything was tough.

Homework. He really did have a lot. And compared to figuring out how to defend the school, doing research about Jack London was going to feel like a vacation.

He and Robert Gerritt had been assigned to work together on this author study, and, as usual, Robert was totally obsessed with getting a perfect grade. So he'd taken charge and immediately volunteered to do most of the reading and most of the writing and most of the oral report. He had given Ben two simpler tasks—making a biographical map of London's life, plus a time line of his published works.

Ben looked over the printouts from his Internet research. Jack London—the guy was amazing. His eye stopped on one article where it said that he'd been an "oyster pirate."

What?

Ben opened his laptop, clicked to Google, and typed in "London AND oyster pirate." Instantly he had his answer. Under cover of night, young Jack London and a gang of thieves had gone on raids to steal fancy oysters from shellfish farms that had been planted in the mud along the shore near San Francisco.

That was a year or so after London had bought his own sailing sloop, and a year or so before he worked his way on a seal hunting ship all the way to Japan.

Which got Ben thinking about ships again. And about life onboard a ship. And about that ship's bell, the one in the school office. And about the clue: *After five bells sound . . .*

Ben navigated back to Google and typed "ship's bell," and then clicked around until he found a list of the bell-ringing patterns that was like the one on the wall in the office. Except this particular listing also showed the different times of day when five bells was rung—two thirty, six thirty, and ten thirty. And it rang for both a.m. times and p.m. times . . . because there were different groups of sailors keeping watch all day and all night. So . . . if you didn't know what *watch* it was when it rang five bells . . . then you couldn't really tell what time it was. Because it rang five bells six times every twenty-four hours. . . .

Pretty confusing.

Ben pulled out a fresh index card and sketched

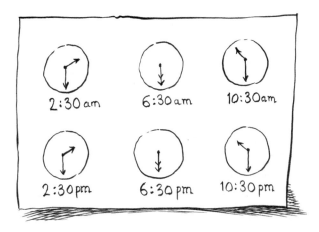

six little clock faces, and he put an hour and a minute hand on each one, then wrote the times below
them.

When he was done, he felt like he understood
what five bells actually meant—at least the time-of-
day part.

Which was progress, right?

But the more he stared at those six clock faces,
the more he thought about the first clue . . . and the
captain . . . and John Vining . . . and Lyman . . . and poor
dead Mr. Keane, and . . . he felt like his head was going
to explode.

So he shut his laptop and tucked the index card

into his pocket and went back to his author study information.

He had *real* homework to do.

And he knew that if he didn't have a clear sketch of Jack London's author time line and also that biographical map before language arts class tomorrow, Robert would kill him—whether Ben had saved his life last Saturday or not.

The author study work took longer than he'd thought it would. Then there were eighteen math problems. Then he had to read the first ten pages of the new chapter in his science book—in case there was another pop quiz.

By the time Ben finished it was late, and he was yawning. Plus, he was hungry again. But it felt good to be done.

He was just about to go down to the kitchen for a snack, when he remembered the white bag from Mrs. Keane. It was right there in his backpack on the bed.

He got out the bag and carefully pulled out that big hunk of chocolate cake. It was sort of smooshed, and when he peeled off the plastic wrap, some of the icing stuck to it. The cake tasted great anyway, even better than it had at the funeral . . . probably because now he was hungrier.

The heavy con-
tainer in the bottom
of the bag had to
be fruit—perfect! Fruit
was juicy, and the thick icing
had made him thirsty. There was even
a plastic fork in the bag.

He pulled out the large cup, pried off the lid, and
stared, his mouth wide open.

There were thirty or forty keys in the cup—keys
of all shapes and sizes. Some were dull brass, some
were silvery, some looked almost new, and others
were worn smooth. And all of them were attached to
one very large ring attached to a belt hook.

He lifted the keys out of the container, and
underneath them was a note, written in blue ink on
a dessert napkin.

*Ben—Roger asked me to give these to
you. He said you'd either make good
use of them and then hand them on
to someone else, or else you'd get to
keep them as a souvenir of a school
that used to be.*

Thanks for being kind to my husband.
Sincerely,
Margaret Keane

The key ring weighed a lot. Ben's head was spinning—so many different locks, all over the school, and every one would open at his command!

Except only a few of the keys were labeled. He pictured himself needing to unlock a door in a hurry, trying key after key after key. A noisy, time-consuming process . . . not to mention illegal.

He sat down to open his laptop, but then stopped, still holding the heavy keys in both hands. Because he'd been all set to tell Jill about this—something exciting, something positive, something possibly very useful . . . but dangerous, too. And what if Lyman figured out who had them? That could get very messy in about a minute. And if he told Jill right now, could just *knowing* about the keys make trouble for her? But he knew she'd want to know, no matter what . . . probably get even madder about everything if he didn't tell her instantly . . . like right this second.

He yawned. Too tired to make a decision. Too tired to think. The keys could wait till tomorrow. Then he would tell her. Tomorrow.

He dropped the keys into his desk drawer and

opened his laptop. There was an e-mail from Jill, a short one:

Nothing online about Vining. Have to check the town library. — J

Ben was relieved. He couldn't deal with new information. Not tonight. This day was over.

He got ready for bed, then walked all the way downstairs to the kitchen for a quick drink of milk. Then he went to the family room to kiss his mom good night, and went to the other end of the couch and gave Nelson a good scratching behind his ears. He went up to the second-floor bathroom to brush his teeth, then walked all the way back up to his room. He shoved his book bag onto the floor and dropped into bed, exhausted.

Instantly he fell asleep—almost. At the last drowsy second, he opened his eyes and tapped the ON button of his alarm clock.

As he did, the big red digital numbers stared him in the face.

It was ten thirty p.m.—five bells.

Ben shut his eyes and imagined he was Jack

London, lying in his hammock on that ship, bound for Japan. His watch was over, and far above, cutting through the sounds of the creaking hull and the sloshing waves, the ship's bell rang.

ding, ding . . . ding, ding . . . ding

CHAPTER 7

Perfect Timing

Ben's best moment on Tuesday was right before school, when he told Jill about Mr. Keane's keys.

Her eyes went wide and round. "His whole huge key ring? No *way*!"

Talking about it, they both agreed that the keys were probably almost useless. But just imagining the possibilities had gotten them laughing, which seemed to snap Jill out of her bad mood—at least temporarily. It had felt like a major victory to Ben.

But the rest of Tuesday? Completely awful and rotten.

To begin with, the whole day was like slogging uphill into an avalanche of schoolwork—

tests, quizzes, reports, new reading assignments—
something extra or new in every single class, even
art. It was as if all the teachers had suddenly realized that in a few short weeks all the sixth graders
would be gone forever, so they'd decided to pile on
the work now while they still had the chance.

But worse than that, there was Lyman.

All day Ben and Jill had seen him everywhere. It
seemed certain now that he was adjusting his janito-
rial work to match up with their daily schedules. At
every turn, there he was, pretending to be busy, but
watching, always glancing the other way at the last
second. It was perfectly clear he was keeping tabs on
both of them.

He had visited both of their homerooms—
to check the sink in the art room, and to change
a lightbulb just above Jill's head in Mrs. Hinman's
room.

Between first and second periods he was sweep-
ing the hall at the south stairwell on the ground
floor, right where Ben and Jill always passed each
other. And when they were taking a quiz together
during their third-period math class, Lyman stopped
in to oil the pencil sharpener—as if it needed it.

He had practically stared at them during lunch in the cafeteria, and when they'd finished eating and gone to the library again, he stopped in to adjust the air register by the east alcove, ten feet from where they were sitting.

And it was the same sort of routine on Wednesday, all morning and right through lunch period. The man was everywhere—as though he'd completely memorized both of their schedules. It had them both constantly on edge, and it ruined their plans for more searching around the school.

The one good thing about it? Jill stopped acting bored. Ben was glad about that—nothing like an attack to get a crew working together. And that's why they did some planning before and after fifth-period social studies. It was time to fight fire with fire.

After school, they walked out the back playground door of the Annex with their jackets and their book bags, right under Lyman's nose. Once outside, they waved to each other and headed for home, Jill going east toward the harbor walk, Ben going west toward School Street.

About five minutes later, they each circled back to school separately. They slipped in the side door

on the north side of the old building, using their hall passes to get past the teachers who were still on bus duty. They met up in the library and ducked into the alcove on the north wall, the spot least visible from the entrance.

It worked. They were completely hidden and totally Lyman-free.

Five minutes later Ben had gotten *A Man of the Sea, A School for the Ages*—the same book that had almost gotten him in trouble Monday morning—from the reserve shelf. They had the large center page of the old book unfolded on the table so they could study the school construction drawings again.

Jill pointed at the upper right-hand corner. "See that drawing of the granite benches outside in the school yard? Do you think the captain would have hidden anything outside? Because all that land is really part of the school, right?"

Before he could answer, Ben heard a noise and looked to his left.

There was Lyman, twenty feet away, emptying a trash basket in the library workroom. He slowly glanced over at them through the glass, a little smile playing at the corners of his mouth. He knew that they'd tried to trick him. And now he knew that *they* knew it hadn't worked. Score one for the bad guy.

"This is creepy," Jill whispered with a shudder. "I feel like he's stalking us."

"That's because he *is*," said Ben. "And he wants us to know it."

Lyman finished emptying the trash, then slowly pushed the rolling trash cart out the doorway into the hall. He was gone, but they knew he'd be back.

"You know what he's doing, tracking us like this?" said Ben. "He's saying, *'I'm* the Keeper of this school— me, Lyman.'"

"Yes." Jill nodded. "And so far, it's working. He's winning, big-time."

Ben felt discouraged too, but he couldn't let Jill know that. If she thought he was losing his nerve, she'd be even more tempted to bail out. And Ben didn't even want to think about what that would mean. They had to stop being scared of Lyman.

"Listen, Jill, I know the guy's a creep, but he's not winning, not even a little bit. And we can't let Lyman get into our heads. He's just trying to spook us. I mean, we know that he doesn't have any of the clues we do—so he's flying blind. He can't really control what we do or what we discover. And . . . you know why he's watching us? Because that's *all* he can do. And we can use that. I know it *feels* rotten, the way he's always around. But it's only a mind game. We've got to remember that we're actually in charge here. And then we can beat him. He thinks we're scared little kids. So what? We're not. We can beat this guy."

"But it's not just Lyman," said Jill. "He's only the part of the problem we bump into every day. The real problem is so much bigger. It's like there are thousands of people, a whole army, and they all want to tear this place down. And we have to fight *all* of them."

"Yes . . . ," Ben said slowly, "but really, it doesn't matter how big the army is—we just have to deal with the enemies at the very front. There's this story called 'Horatius at the Bridge' in a book my dad got when he was a kid. It's about this soldier in ancient Rome when this huge attacking army was trying to capture the city. Horatius's part of the Roman army got trapped on the wrong side of the Tiber River, and they needed to retreat back to Rome across this narrow bridge. His soldiers panicked and tried to crush their way onto the bridge, and some enemy soldiers joined the crowd and tried to get across too. But when Horatius got to the bridge, instead of running across it, he pulled out his sword and turned around and started fighting the enemies, and that inspired two other soldiers to join him. These three guys let their own men retreat across the bridge, but they killed the invaders. And because the bridge was narrow, it didn't matter how big the enemy army was— only the first two or three men could fight at a time, and Horatius and his friends kept killing whoever got close. When all the good guys got across safely, they began to rip out the bridge behind Horatius, and the two other soldiers with him ran and jumped across the gap. But Horatius stayed and kept fighting until the whole bridge was destroyed and the city was safe. It's a true story."

"Really?" said Jill. "And Horatius got killed?"

"Nope. He got hit by a spear, and at the last second he turned and dove into the river. He swam all the way across with his armor and all his weapons, and he survived. His wounds were so bad that he couldn't stay in the army. But he was a hero, and the citizens of Rome gave him his own land, and even made a bronze statue to honor him."

Jill was quiet a moment.

"And now it's you and me," she said. "At the bridge."

"That's right," said Ben. "We don't have to defeat a whole army all at once. If we fight smart and we don't panic, we'll be good. So . . . Lyman's not here, and we've got some time. How about we look at your notes from Monday and Tuesday?"

Jill nodded and pulled out the slim three-ring binder where she had begun filing everything.

They looked at the first page together in silence. It was the text from the copper plate, and at the bottom Jill had traced the outline of the big key. Ben nodded when he was done reading, and Jill flipped the page.

The second sheet had the clue for the first safeguard written across the top, with two columns underneath: possible bells listed on the left, possible places to sit listed on the right.

The next page had three photos, printed out from an e-mail Ben had sent to Jill on Tuesday night: the bell from HMS *Safeguard*, the plaque about the sea battle, and the plaque showing the bell patterns. And at the bottom of this page, Jill had taped the index card Ben had used to sketch the different times of day when five bells were rung aboard a ship.

And that was it. Only three pages. No conclusions. No findings.

"Well, Horatius," Jill said, "you have to admit

things look pretty bad." She flopped back against the cushions that lined the alcove bench. "We *have* nothing, we *know* nothing, and there are hundreds of places, *thousands* of places around this building where things could be hidden. It's hopeless."

Ben didn't know what to say. He kept staring at the third page of the notebook. He could feel Jill's discouragement again. Even worse, he felt the same way. He glanced up cautiously, expecting to see defeat in her face.

What he saw was curiosity.

She was looking at a spot on the wall of the alcove, about two feet above his head.

"That is the *biggest* pocket watch I have ever seen."

Ben twisted around to see what she was staring at. She was right. He got to his knees on the bench for a closer look.

The thing was made of silver, but it sure wasn't a pocket watch. It was huge, more than five inches across. It was inside a case made of beveled glass and dark wood, which was fastened onto the wall with four metal bolts. Below the timepiece, a small brass plate was tacked to the wood of the case.

THIS LONGITUDE CLOCK BELONGED

TO CAPTAIN REYNOLD HARDCASTLE,

AND WAS TAKEN FROM HIS SHIP IN

BARCLAY BAY AS A PRIZE OF BATTLE.

Ben sat back down. "It's just a chronometer."

"Okay . . . ," Jill said. Then, two seconds later, "I give up. What's a chronometer?"

"A really accurate clock used on a ship for figuring out longitude, which is east/west location. If you know where you were when you started sailing, and you know how long you've been sailing, then you can figure out your longitude. Except it's more complicated than that."

"Ah, yes—of course," said Jill with mock respect. "I keep forgetting that you are the Wizard of the Waves, the ultimate sailor boy."

Ben ignored the sarcasm.

Then she leaned forward and squinted. "Notice anything strange about that thing?" She seemed excited, but Ben was pretty sure she was setting up a joke, getting ready to tease him again. He didn't take the bait.

"Nope."

"The hands are pointing down—six thirty!" She tapped the clock drawings Ben had made on the index card. "Five bells!"

Ben scrambled back to his knees.

The hands were showing six thirty, and even the second hand was pointing straight down. And up close, Ben saw an inscription in a thin, curlicue script along the bottom edge of the clock:

A gift for my loyal friend, Reynold Hardcastle, Captain, HMS Safeguard

Five bells on a clock from the *Safeguard*—and the hands were pointing straight down . . . at a bench!

Ben felt like he'd been hit by lightning. He turned and locked eyes with Jill across the table, just for one thrilling second.

She grinned. "Time to sit down!"

"Quick," he said, "spread your jacket across the back of that chair—no, let it hang down close to the floor . . . good." He arranged things as he talked. "And then this chair goes right beside it, and—hand me your backpack, will you? That goes on the floor right there . . . and that should hide me. In case someone looks this way. Or if Lyman comes back."

He dropped his backpack onto the floor, glanced around quickly, then slid forward and disappeared under the table. Reaching across to his book bag, he unzipped the outer pocket and found his flashlight.

The section of the bench directly below the clock was about three feet wide, and he scooched around on his back until he could look straight up at the bottom of the seat.

He turned on the flashlight and played the beam across the wooden slats. Nothing obvious. Just three darkened oak boards, two of them wide and one narrow, running side to side.

He adjusted the light into a tight, focused shaft.

"How's it look up there?" he whispered.

"All clear," Jill whispered back. "Spot anything yet?"

"Mostly a lot of chewed gum."

"Gross!"

And it was. Ben was nose to nose with at least twenty wads of the stuff—pink, green, gray, white, mostly along the front edge. But he tried to look past all that and forced himself to concentrate on the wood. If something was there, he was going to find it.

Starting along the wall at the rear of the bench, he moved the light beam slowly and methodically, back and forth, back and forth. It took more than a minute for his inspection to reach the front edge of the bench. He was being careful—and it paid off.

Right where the bench frame joined one of the supporting legs, he saw tiny dots on the front slat. He reached up and brushed away some cobwebs. Could that be . . . ? No. But he angled his flashlight so the beam hit the wood from a different angle. And there it was . . . a familiar pattern.

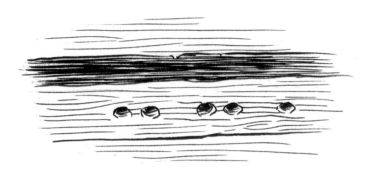

The five little dots had been pushed into the hard oak by something sharp, maybe the point of an awl—five bells!

Excited now, he scanned the front slat near the leg on the opposite side, brushed aside the spiderwebs, and . . . more dots, the same grouping, five bells. And just below those dots, it looked like someone had drilled a neat little hole into the frame of the bench.

Ben aimed his light at the opposite side again—nothing. But he reached up anyway and used his sleeve to brush off the rest of the dust and cobwebs. And there it was, a second hole, same size, same location just below the dots! No way was that a coincidence. . . .

"Jill! I need something thin and round—got anything made of metal?"

"Like what?" she asked.

"I don't know—maybe a small nail?"

"I *think* I left my handy bag of nails at home today."

More sarcasm. But Ben saw her leaning down, heard her rummaging around in her backpack.

"Um . . . how about a ballpoint pen?"

"Too thick," he whispered. "Do you have any paper clips?"

"Um . . . yeah, I've got two, a big one and a little one."

"Great! Toss 'em here—thanks."

Ben held the flashlight with his teeth and quickly bent each clip so a stiff piece of wire stuck out straight.

Holding a clip in each hand, he fitted the ends into the holes and pushed.

No give at all. He pushed harder and felt a little movement, then . . . *click*. The front edge of the slat dropped onto his fingers.

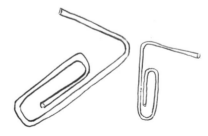

"Ow!" He nearly lost his grip on the paper clips.

"Shhh," Jill hissed. "What happened?"

"Pinched my fingers—this board . . . Hey, wait a second! There's something in there!"

Ben wriggled out from under the bench, yanked both paper clips free, and pulled the front edge of the slat the rest of the way down.

Jill kicked his leg. "Lyman! He's at the doorway, walking over to the front desk!"

"Quick," Ben said, "give me your notebook!"

She slipped it under the table, and he grabbed it.

"Hurry!" she said. "He's going into the workroom again!"

There was another sharp *click*, and a second later Ben was sitting on the bench across the table from her, a pencil in his hand, eyes on the papers in front of him, looking almost bored.

Out of the corner of his eye Ben could see the workroom. Sure enough, Lyman was inside, facing them through the glass, a rag in one hand and a spray bottle in the other. The window was perfectly clean, but he sprayed a little, then wiped a little, sprayed a little more, wiped a little more, and he kept that up for about two minutes—just long enough to send his message. Ben turned and glared at him.

Jill kicked him again. "Stop staring, Benjamin . . . stop it. *Now!*"

Ben didn't want to stop. He wanted to lock eyes and have a good old-fashioned stare-down with the tiger—see who blinked first.

But he knew Jill's way was smarter, so he brought his eyes back to the table.

After what seemed like an eternity, Jill said, "He's gone." Then, breathlessly, "Did you actually find something?"

Ben whispered, "I actually did!"

CHAPTER 8

Tick Tock

"Let me see what you found!" Jill hissed. "I want to see it!"

"Quiet!" whispered Ben. "Come to this side." He was sitting on the bench, right below the chronometer.

Jill scooted around the end of the table and slid in close to his elbow. "Okay, open it up!"

Ben was breathing too fast. He pressed both hands flat on Jill's notebook and tried to take a deep breath, nice and slow—and he couldn't. He felt a little faint, and in his mind he kept shouting, *We found the first safeguard! We found it!*

Ben wanted to slow everything down, but Jill nudged him.

"Come on!"

He opened the notebook cover, then flipped past a few sheets of lined paper. And there it was— a document, a piece of vellum or parchment about eight inches square, a little yellowed, but the writing was dark and clear. It looked like some sort of small round sticker or seal was fastened on the lower right-hand corner.

"A letter?" Jill asked. "That's *it*?"

"Just read," Ben said. "It has to be important, right?"

He held up the paper carefully by the edges so they could both see it clearly.

Be this known to all men:
I am Captain Duncan Oakes, resident of
Edgeport, Massachusetts, and I do hereby
proclaim and avow that the bearer of this
one and only codicil to my last will and
testament, upon its presentation to the
proper legal authority, at that moment
does become the full, complete and permanent
owner of the building known as the
Captain Duncan Oakes School, including
all of its surrounding property as recorded
in the Essex County Registry of Deeds.
The transfer of ownership shall remain in

Be this known to all men:

I am Captain Duncan Oakes, resident of Edgeport, Massachusetts, and I do hereby proclaim and avow that the bearer of this one and only codicil to my last will and testament, upon its presentation to the proper legal authority, at that moment does become the full, complete, and permanent owner of the building known as the Captain Duncan Oakes School, including all of its surrounding property as recorded in the Essex County Registry of Deeds. This transfer of ownership shall remain in effect so long as the bearer and any successors continue to secure the use of said building and grounds as a public school to benefit the children of Edgeport. Should said building and grounds ever be put to other use, then full ownership shall pass immediately and irrevocably to the Commonwealth of Massachusetts.

Being of sound mind and body, I now hereunto set my hand on this fifteenth day of August in the year seventeen hundred and eighty-three.

Duncan Oakes
Witness: John Vining

Jill whispered, "Did the captain—"

"Shh!" Ben lifted one finger. "Not done yet." A few seconds later he lowered the finger and whispered, *"Wow!"*

Jill continued, "So, that's the captain's own handwriting?"

Ben nodded. "Looks that way. Written in 1783 with a quill pen—amazing!" He laid the document down and reached for his camera. "I've got to get a shot of this."

"What—*now*?" said Jill.

"Absolutely, for documentation. Archaeologists, field historians, anthropologists—everybody does it. Whenever you find something, you take a picture— or at least make a sketch. We *should* have gotten photos when we found the key and the copper plate up on the third floor. Because if—"

"Okay, okay," said Jill. "Let me clear some space." She picked up the document, and as she started to set it on the bench, the small round seal popped loose from the bottom corner and fluttered to the floor under the table.

"Hey!" Ben glared at her. "Here, I'll hold it. Pick that little piece up *very* carefully—and hurry.

Lyman could come back any second."

Jill stooped down and then handed the seal to Ben.

A Man of the Sea was still spread out on the table, and Jill quickly folded the large double-sized pages inward, shut the book, and set it to one side. She shoved her notebook out of the way.

"There," she said, "and be sure the flash is turned off."

Ben set the document down on the dark wood, and after he put the round seal back in its place, he snapped a picture.

Jill leaned down and squinted at the seal. Then she reached over and picked it up, holding it like it was a rare butterfly. "Is that some kind of writing on this thing?"

Ben peered over her shoulder. "Can't tell—too small. I can check it out later with a magnifying glass. Here . . ."

He held out his hand and when Jill passed it over, he tucked the seal carefully between the pages of his social studies book.

Bending over the document again, he said, "Any idea what a 'codicil' is?"

"No—I'll grab a dictionary!"

Ben was glad to see Jill so excited—he was too. It was like they had this fish on the line, and it was definitely hooked, but they couldn't tell how big it was yet.

A minute later Jill read the definition out loud: "'codicil: an addition to a will.'"

"So that means . . . hmm . . . ," Ben started again. "So, it means that . . ."

Jill began talking so fast she could barely get the words out. "It *means* that this paper wipes out a part of Captain Oakes's *old* will, the part about giving the school to the town. And if you handed this piece of paper to someone like a judge, you would automatically become the new owner of the school and all the land around it. At least, I *think* that's what it means . . . and if that's true, then it's no wonder the captain hid it so carefully!"

"Wow!" said Ben. "I mean, this could change *everything*, right? The town, the heirs, Glennley, everybody gets totally blown away by one little piece of paper!"

He paused. "But it kind of seems impossible, doesn't it?"

"I don't know," said Jill. "That's a question for a lawyer."

"So, should we find one?"

"Well . . ." Jill thought a moment. "It would have to be a lawyer we really trusted. Because when it says 'The *bearer* of this document'? I think *that* means that whoever actually has their hands on *that* piece of paper is the new owner. And, like, what would stop some shady lawyer from taking this away from us and walking it right over to the courthouse?"

"But," Ben said, "no matter what, the new owner would still have to keep using the place as a school . . . right?"

"Yes," said Jill, "that's right—or else the state of Massachusetts would suddenly own a big piece of waterfront land in Edgeport."

"What happened here?"

They both looked up, startled.

Ms. Shubert, the assistant librarian, had come up from their blind side. Ben quickly put out his hand to try to cover the codicil.

"Ahh . . . I see," she said, picking up *A Man of the Sea*. "Well, this happens all the time with these old books."

Ben and Jill exchanged quick glances—what was she talking about?

Ms. Shubert went on, "I can't tell you how many times whole pages have fallen out. And those glued-in illustrations are the worst. But I'm sure I can make a quick repair, and Mrs. Sinclair will never have to know." Nodding at the codicil, she said, "Do you remember what page that was on?"

Ben stuttered, thinking fast, "Um . . . I—I think it was right at the very end of the book. On a blank page all by itself. It—it just fell out."

"Well, it's easy enough to fix." She lifted the book's thick back cover, then picked up the document, tucked it inside, and let the cover drop shut. "But try to be more careful next time, okay? Listen, I'm leaving in about five minutes, so you two have to run along now."

As Ben and Jill watched, Ms. Shubert whisked the book away . . . along with the codicil.

Ben whispered, "This is terrible!" Jill nodded glumly.

The assistant librarian marched right into the workroom and set the volume on a long table. On her way out, she shut off the lights, turned the LOCK button on the back of the knob, then pulled the door shut behind her.

Stunned and silent, Jill and Ben gathered up their things.

It wasn't until they were all the way out the front door of the school and standing by the water's edge that either of them could speak.

"If she *reads* that piece of paper, we're sunk," said Ben.

"And if Lyman swipes that book again, we're double-sunk," Jill added.

"But," Ben added in the most cheerful voice he could manage, "all we have to do is take the document out of the book tomorrow—she said she was going do a quick repair. So . . . I'll just get it back. No big deal." He sounded more upbeat than he felt.

"Right," Jill said, ". . . unless she takes a good look at it and sees it's not a printed photograph. If she figures out what it really is, then we just gave Ms. Shubert an original document that's worth about fifty million dollars."

That idea shut both of them up. Out beyond the bay a high-speed ferry blasted its air horn. The deep tone echoed across the water until it was swallowed up by the breeze and the lapping waves.

"You know . . . ," Ben said, "maybe that thing is actually in a very safe hiding place—almost as safe as it was under the bench." He wheeled to face her. "I mean, Lyman had that book all last weekend and then brought it back. So he's done with it. Robert already got what he wanted out of it, and Ms. Shubert's got a million other things to do, so she just fastens the loose sheet onto a blank page and sticks the book back in the reference section. And there it sits, safe and sound."

Ben pulled his camera out of his pocket. "Meanwhile, we can print a *copy* and show it to a lawyer. And ask what it means. If it turns out that there's a way this thing could really stop the Glennley plans, we know where to get our hands on the original." Ben began talking faster and faster, shaking the camera as if it were the actual document. "I mean, this could really *work*—just like you said! It could shut Glennley down cold, like *tomorrow*—BAM! Game over, case closed—it really could! Right? So we need to talk to a lawyer, fast!"

Jill hesitated. "Well . . . I guess so. Maybe. But how do we know we can trust a lawyer?"

Ben said, "I thought lawyers have to swear to keep everything a secret, all the stuff their customers tell them—didn't I hear that somewhere?"

"I think so," she said, "but I'm not sure we could even talk to one, not without a parent being there. And stop shouting and shaking your arms around. Somebody's going to think you've flipped out."

Ben talked more quietly but just as fast. "All I'm saying is, we don't have any time to waste. We have to figure out exactly what that codicil means, one way or the other, right now. And if it's useless, then we jump right in and start looking for the *next* safeguard, just that quick."

Jill made a face. "That's a depressing thought."

"*Depressing?* How come? Look," he said, "we just *proved* that the safeguards are for real, *and* that we can actually find them! Which is really good news! So, if we have to find some other safeguards, then we will. But the great thing is, we *might* not even need to look! If we can talk to a lawyer, like, this whole attack could be over *tomorrow*—and *that's* completely *awesome*! We just have to talk to a lawyer. Right?"

Jill nodded. "Well, sure."

All her excitement, all the enthusiasm he had

seen just a few minutes ago was gone, vanished. Ben stared at Jill, puzzled by the look in her eyes.

Then he suddenly knew what he was looking at.

"What are you so scared about?"

Jill's face twisted with emotion . . . but just for half a second.

"What are you talking about?" she snapped. "I'm not *scared* about talking to some lawyer. Go ahead and print out a copy of the document, and I'll try to find one who'll meet with us. And maybe it'll be someone we can trust. I totally agree—we've got to move fast, see if that document is a game changer. And we also have to check and make sure Ms. Shubert actually puts the original codicil in the back of that book. And we have to be extra sure Lyman doesn't catch on that there's anything unusual happening. But we definitely need to talk to a lawyer, like, tomorrow—absolutely."

"Right," said Ben.

"Okay," Jill said, "good. So I'll go home and start Googling for a lawyer, okay? And I'll let you know if I have any news. Anything else I should do?"

"No, I don't think so," he said.

"Good—see you later."

"See you later," said Ben.

Jill turned quickly and walked south along the harbor path.

Ben watched her go. She was walking too fast, like she wanted to get away from him.

It had been a good speech—Jill Acton, the hard-hitting team player, tough and organized. Was she scared about meeting with a lawyer? Not one bit. Ben believed that part.

Jill probably thought she had fooled him completely, made him think she wasn't afraid at all. Of anything.

Ben knew better. He had seen it in her eyes, just for a second—real fear. About something else. Something still hidden.

He wanted to help, and she wouldn't let him. And there was nothing he could do about it, not until she asked.

But when would that be?

He knew how stubborn Jill was. And proud. She could probably go on like this forever, pretending nothing was wrong.

He didn't have forever. Time was running out.

CHAPTER 9

Messages

By the time Ben got home, he'd managed to put Jill out of his mind, at least temporarily. He was back in the Keepers hunt, and he wanted to get a close look at the little seal that had fallen off the codicil.

His mom hadn't arrived home yet, so he trotted all the way up to his attic room, dug his social studies book out of his bag, and thumbed through the pages until he found the seal.

He set it on his desk and clicked on his bright study lamp.

Ink, lots of it. Splotches and marks and blots all over the place. But he was pretty sure there was writing, too. He took a small magnifying glass from his desk drawer—yes, definitely writing, but the magnifier wasn't strong enough. Time to go high-tech.

He got out his camera, took a close-up picture, then plugged it into his laptop and imported the image onto the screen.

Still tiny, still just a bunch of inky scratches.

So he enlarged the image on the screen—200 percent . . . 300 percent . . . and at 400 percent larger, he could read something.

On an index card, he wrote down exactly what he saw:

ABput

thinge

ahind

shleff

at window

The "thinge" and the "at window" parts seemed clear enough . . . but "ahind"?

He enlarged the image a little more and told his computer to sharpen the image. The computer obeyed . . . and there it was—message received!

He grabbed his phone and hit Jill's number on speed dial.

"Hi."

"Hey, guess what? That seal that fell off the codicil? It wasn't a seal at all! It's a tiny little note: 'AB put things ahind shelf at window.' AB—that has to be Abigail Baynes, the same girl whose name is on the copper plate. She wanted to get in on the Keepers action, so she hid some stuff in the library, and then slipped her own message in with the codicil! Cool, huh?"

"'Ahind'?" said Jill. "What's that mean?"

"'Afore' means 'before'—I'm sure of that. So 'ahind' must be the same as 'behind.' Boy, she was rotten at spelling, and it looks like the paper she wrote on came from a scrap pile, but her message got through. And now we've got something else to look for!"

"Terrific," Jill said, her voice dripping with sarcasm. "Just what we need."

If they'd been in the same room, Ben might have punched Jill on the arm for that, so it was a good thing she was half a mile away. But he lost his temper all the same.

"Okay, fine. Well, I am so *very, very* sorry to

bother you with my boring historical interruptions. I'll let you know when I find something worth your valuable time. Nice talking to you."

He hung up.

His phone rang just seconds later. It was her.

He let it ring four times, then picked up and pretended to be his own voice-mail message. "This is Ben—say something," followed by his best fake *"Beeeep."*

Jill started to talk, leaving him a message.

"Ben—sorry . . . it really is cool, what Abigail wrote. And when you were talking about it, I could really imagine her, figuring out how to leave something of her own there. With the other thing." She paused, and Ben heard her breathing. "So anyway, I'm really sorry. It's just that, right now . . . it's . . . well, anyway, I hope you get this. . . . Talk to you later. . . . Bye."

Ben let the line go dead. Her message was over.

So many messages. On a round scrap of paper, on a neat vellum sheet, on a copper plate, on a gold coin in his pocket, even on a big key.

Then this newest message, only seconds old. It started at Jill's lips, shot through her phone, flashed through space, bounced off a satellite, and made vibrations in his ear. In his heart, too, if he was honest with himself.

He wasn't mad at her.

He just wanted the old Jill back. It was important, for lots of reasons.

And really, if she hadn't been sarcastic about it, he might have admitted that she had a point. Did they need someone sending them on a new treasure hunt right now? Not really. This newest two-hundred-year-old message would have to move to the end of the line.

Ben shut his laptop. He rummaged around in his desk drawer until he found a clear plastic sleeve, a baseball card protector. He flexed it open and slipped the tiny message inside. Safe and sound. Preserved. An artifact.

They would have to catch up with Abigail later.

It was time to deal with first things first.

CHAPTER 10

Copper Beech

Ben blinked a few times, not sure where he was. He noticed a kind of chemical odor. Then he realized that the side of his face was jammed flat against his social studies book, and what he smelled was ink and shiny paper. He blinked again and noticed the digital clock over by his bed—9:23. He'd left two chapters of reading as the last thing to do tonight—a mistake.

He peeled his face off the page, yawned, and leaned back in his chair, gradually focusing his eyes. He saw the window on the slanted ceiling of his room, then the night sky beyond it. The moon was bright, not quite full, with clouds slipping past from east to west—a brisk onshore breeze.

He stood up on his desk chair and pushed the window open a few inches, then stretched up higher so he could get his nose close to the crack. He pulled in a deep breath of the cool night air. The ocean was almost half a mile east, but when the wind was right, the whole neighborhood smelled like the beach.

As he took a second breath, his cell phone rang. He reached into his pocket and nearly lost his balance. Catching the back of his desk chair just in time, he stepped down, then dropped backward onto his bed. He flipped the phone open and glanced at the screen—Jill.

Maybe she'd found out something about a lawyer.

"Hey," he said.

No response. Ben sat straight up on his bed, took another quick look at the screen. The connection seemed fine.

"Jill? You there? Hello?"

"Can't talk," she whispered.

"What's going on?" Ben heard rustling noises. He strained, trying to hear more . . . nothing. "Are you okay?"

She whispered, "I'm at the big copper beech on the south lawn of the school. Bring your Swiss Army knife. Also Band-Aids."

The line went dead.

Ben jumped to his feet, heart pounding, instantly wide awake. He grabbed the small flashlight from his backpack, then found his Swiss Army knife in his desk drawer and stuffed it in his pocket. He rushed down the attic stairs and heard water running into the tub of the second-floor bathroom.

"Mom?" he called through the door.

The water stopped. "What, honey?"

"I'm gonna take Nelson out for a run around the block."

Ben pictured her frowning.

"I think it's pretty late, isn't it?"

"It's not even ten yet," he said, then quickly added, "Besides, nobody messes with a person who's got a dog. I need the exercise—too much sitting still today. I'll be fine."

"All right," she said, "but be careful."

"Always am," he said, and then shot down the front hall stairs two at a time.

The first-aid stuff was in the wall cabinet of

the powder room off the kitchen. He grabbed a handful of Band-Aids, the largest ones.

He got the leash off the table by the front door and gave a short whistle. "Here, Nelson—out!"

The corgi's little legs churned and skittered all over the hardwood floor, and he yipped and danced as Ben fastened the leash.

"Back in a few," he hollered up the stairs. The water was running again.

Ben took off running east along Walnut Street, and Nelson's claws clicked away on the sidewalk beside him. The clouds had blotted out the moon, so he used the flashlight to be sure of his footing between the streetlamps.

As he ran, he tried not to worry about Jill, but he couldn't help it. Why was she in the school yard this late? And why did she want him to bring his knife? Asking for Band-Aids—that had to mean she'd gotten hurt . . . but how? And why hadn't she been able to talk to him?

He crossed School Street, and at the gate to the school property, he ignored the sign that said NO DOGS ALLOWED. The pathway through the parkland was lit by lampposts every hundred feet or so, but he didn't want to be seen. He flipped off his flashlight and steered to the right. He also slowed to a walk, trying to get his breathing under control, trying not to feel panicked, and trying not to run into any trees or granite park benches.

He knew exactly which tree Jill meant. The big copper beech was more than a hundred and fifty years old, and it towered above a grove of oaks and maples in the area directly south of the school. Its smooth gray bark always reminded Ben of the giant World War II battleship he and his dad had toured on a visit to Fall River. The trunk of the copper beech was almost twenty feet around, with a huge rack of branches that started close to the ground—perfect for climbing. Anyone brave enough to keep going higher got an incredible view of the bay and the coastline.

NO DOGS ALLOWED

Looking up, Ben could see the faint edges of the tree's canopy outlined against the clouds. He shortened Nelson's leash and moved ahead slowly. When he reached the trunk, he started around it toward his left.

"Jill?" he whispered.

Halfway around he whispered again. "Ji—"

He stumbled on something and nearly fell to the ground, then stepped on something else and went down in a heap, making a huge racket. Nelson let out a yelp.

"*Shhh!* Stay there," Jill whispered. "I'm coming down."

Ben rubbed his knee, and moments later he heard Jill drop to the ground from a branch on the other side of the tree. "Are you all right?" she whispered.

"Yeah, I'm good. And . . . you're okay?"

"I'll be fine."

"'Cause I brought some Band-Aids."

"Good. But first you have to help me toss this stuff into the bay."

"What stuff?"

"The stakes," she said. "You tripped on them."

"What!"

"*Shhh!*"

Ben fumbled for his flashlight, shielded half the lens, and clicked it on. The dim light showed he was next to a huge heap of stakes, their pointed ends still covered with moist earth.

For the past week Ben and Jill had watched teams of surveyors carefully laying out the new theme park on the school property, marking where the gates and parking lots would be, where the foundations for the new buildings and the rides would be dug, and spraying big red *X*s on all the trees that were in the way. Dozens of the ribboned stakes bristled on the school grounds, each carefully placed by men and women wearing hard hats, each driven into the ground with a hammer.

"Are you *nuts*?" he hissed. "You could go to *jail* for this!"

"Not if I don't get caught. Are you going to help me or not?"

"Help you do what?"

"Throw these into the water."

"That's pollution!"

"Do you have a better idea? Besides, they're just wood—they'll sink pretty soon, or get washed up on some beach. C'mon."

She bent down and began loading her arms with the four-foot-long stakes. Ben felt like he had to help.

He took one of the stakes, pushed it into the ground, and looped Nelson's leash around it.

"Stay." The corgi lay down and yawned.

Ben and Jill each picked up ten or twelve stakes and headed toward the water. The last fifty feet or so were the most dangerous, because the trees thinned out and the harbor walk was lit by lampposts—but that also made it easy to scan both directions. When it was all clear, they both sprinted to the seawall, tossed the stakes into Barclay Bay, then ran back into the darkness.

It took three trips like that, and on the third one Nelson ran with them so that every last stake was thrown into the bay. The light swell from the onshore breeze had kept most of the sticks close to the seawall, and they made a soggy clicking sound as they hit against one another. Ben knew that when the tide turned in an hour or so, they'd all be pulled out to sea.

Back at the big tree, Jill said, "Now I need those Band-Aids. But first the Swiss Army knife. Can I hold the flashlight?"

Covering most of the brightness with her left hand, she aimed a tiny spot of light onto her right palm.

Ben gasped. It was red and raw, and the reason was obvious. Jill had yanked up each of those stakes with her bare hands.

"See the slivers?" she said.

"Yeah, I see 'em." Ben felt slightly sick, but he wasn't going to let Jill know that. He pulled the tweezers from their place in the red handle of his knife. "This is gonna hurt. . . ."

Ben held Jill's hand tightly and began poking around for the first splinter. He felt her tense up when he hit it. "Sorry."

She took a deep breath and held it. Ben got a good grip with the tweezers and yanked it out—about half an inch of jagged oak. The hole in her hand began bleeding right away, and Ben remembered that that was good—it helped clean the cut. But the sight of the blood made him feel even woozier.

Jill let her breath out. "Good," she said. "See that one? There, near my pinkie."

"Yeah—got it."

The second and third slivers were much smaller, so there was more digging around. Jill flinched, but she didn't make a sound. Ben was impressed, but he wasn't surprised. Nothing about this girl would ever surprise him again.

"Is that it?" he asked.

"Think so—thanks. Do you have those Band-Aids?"

"Sure."

Ben gently smoothed on three of them, edge to edge, which completely covered her palm. Her hand seemed so small compared to his.

As he finished, she handed him his flashlight and asked, "How did you get out of the house?"

"Walking the dog. But my mom'll probably call any second. How about you?"

"Just sneaked out. My mom and dad were . . . downstairs. And . . . I got the idea of pulling out all the stakes, and I just had to come and do it. I had to . . . and I did."

Ben knew that wasn't the whole story, it couldn't be. But he'd ask for details later.

"Listen," he said, "I'll walk home with you, okay?"

"No, you'd better take Nelson back. I'll be fine. Thanks for coming so fast. And I hope you don't get in trouble. Really, thanks."

"Anytime," Ben said. And he meant it.

"Good to know," said Jill. It sounded like she meant that, too.

"So, see you tomorrow," he said.

"Right," she said, "tomorrow."

Ben stood still in the dark beneath the big tree and watched Jill's shadow until she reached the brightly lit path. She turned with a smile and waved with her bandaged hand, then set off at a trot.

Ben whispered, "C'mon, Nelson. Let's get you home."

CHAPTER 11

An Honest Lawyer

It was Thursday, almost four o'clock in the afternoon. Ben and Jill sat in the waiting room just before their appointment with a lawyer, a woman named Amanda Burgess.

Back when everyone first discovered that the Glennley Group was trying to buy the school property, Mrs. Burgess had attended some town meetings as the attorney for the Edgeport Historical Society. Jill's mom was a member, and she had kept records of all those meetings—which was how Jill had found the lawyer's name.

When she called and asked Mrs. Burgess for an interview, Jill had explained how she and a partner were doing a social studies project on the history of the Oakes School, and that they wanted to ask her some questions about the captain's original will. All perfectly true. That was also what both of them had told their moms, to explain why they would be coming home late after school.

Leaning back in a wide leather armchair, Ben shut his eyes and reviewed the plan. It wasn't complicated: Ask some questions about the captain's will, and then ask some more questions about how the Glennley Group got past that will. The rest of the plan depended on the way the lawyer answered the questions, and whether she seemed like an honest person—really, really honest.

Jill had seemed a lot more like herself at school today, more friendly, not quite as edgy. She'd apologized in person about the way she'd reacted on the phone last night, about the Abigail Baynes thing. She'd also thanked him again for meeting her at the copper beech tree. That had made it feel like a better day, but again, Lyman had shadowed both of them everywhere. Another school day was gone, and they'd made no real progress with any searching at all.

He still hadn't asked Jill what had made her suddenly run out into the dark last night and yank up all those stakes. When they had noticed the surveying crew stomping around the grounds outside during lunch recess, Jill had nodded toward them and smiled a little, but other than that, nothing. She'd seemed hesitant and distant for days, then *boom*—she went and did something crazy and intense. And this meeting felt sort of the same way. Jill had insisted that they needed to come and talk with this lawyer right away, today.

Ben took a deep breath and let it out slowly, trying to calm down. It didn't help. He still felt like there was a rope twisted around his stomach—with Captain Oakes pulling on one end, and Jill pulling on the other.

The receptionist's phone buzzed, and a moment later the young man at the desk said, "Miss Acton, Mr. Pratt? Attorney Burgess will see you now. Go right through that door."

As Ben walked into the office, the brightness made him blink—six large windows faced east and south. They were on the third floor of an old rope factory, just a block away from where Jill lived. The land sloped uphill from the bay, so the water and the coastline seemed to stretch on forever. Off toward the south, Ben could see four or five little Optimist sailboats, tacking and making turns around a practice buoy. He instantly spotted USA 222 on one of the sails—Robert's boat. He was out there sailing on a beautiful afternoon, getting prepped for the next round of races. It almost ruined the view.

"Jill, Benjamin, welcome."

Mrs. Burgess smiled and stood up from behind a large desk covered with ten or twelve neat stacks of file folders. Ben guessed she was about the same height as his mom, five-one or five-two. But older—dark brown hair with some gray here and there. She was attractive, but not at all glamorous. She had on a white blouse, and her jacket and pants were dark blue. Businesslike, in a friendly sort of way. The bracelet on her right wrist wasn't fancy, but it looked expensive. Same with her wedding rings and her wristwatch. She stepped forward quickly and shook hands with Jill, then with him.

Ben noticed that Jill didn't flinch when the lawyer squeezed her injured hand. There were only two Band-Aids on her palm today, smaller ones.

She led them toward a couch and four chairs

arranged around a low table by the windows. "Let's sit over here."

When they were settled, she said, "So you're working on a history project, correct?"

"Yes," Jill said. "We're trying to find out as much as we can about the Oakes School."

Ben nodded. "Especially since it's going to be torn down soon."

A quick frown darkened Mrs. Burgess's face. "It's quite something, isn't it? I've lived in Edgeport most of my life, and I loved going to that school. And to think it'll be gone"—she snapped her fingers—"just like that. Hard to imagine." Then she flashed a bright smile. "Well, the future keeps coming, whether we're ready for it or not. So, how can I help? Jill said you two had some questions about Captain Oakes and his will."

They hadn't rehearsed how this part was going to go, but Mrs. Burgess was looking at him, so Ben nodded. "That's right. I looked at a copy of Captain Oakes's will, at the part where he gave his building and the land to be a school, and also where he said his gravestone should be right on the school playground. So I was wondering, was that unusual? I mean, did other people back then write things like that in their wills?"

Mrs. Burgess nodded. "Absolutely. It happened back then, and it still happens today. Lots of people have made all sorts of strange provisions in their wills—you hear about it on the news sometimes, where someone leaves a large sum of money to a poodle, or where a person requires that everyone wear a special sort of costume if they want to attend his funeral—lots of odd requirements. And people also leave land and money to schools or universities all the time. So those aspects of the captain's will are actually quite common." She paused. "The unusual part is the way Captain Oakes tried to protect his wishes out into the future. And he thought he had planned it all out perfectly, by getting the town of Edgeport involved. He must have felt sure that the town officials and citizens would never want to give up such a fine school, and in such a wonderful location, and simply let ownership pass to his heirs."

As she said that last bit, Ben noticed some emotion in her voice.

Jill must have picked up on that too.

"Were you surprised," Jill asked, "when the town

council made that offer to the captain's heirs, to pay them for giving up all their rights?"

"Surprised? Honestly, no. After twenty-seven years of practicing law, nothing surprises me anymore." She stopped, thought a second, then added, "However, it did make me quite sad."

"Well," Jill went on carefully, "I did wonder if there was some special reason you worked for the Historical Society, when they were trying to stop the deal."

"Yes," she said, "but by that time it was too late. And then I had to remove myself from the whole business anyway. But you two probably know all about *that*." And her voice suddenly seemed sharp, almost sarcastic.

It caught Ben off guard.

Jill was confused too. She shook her head. "Um . . . I don't know what you're . . . um . . ."

Ben had never seen Jill so flustered.

Mrs. Burgess looked first into Jill's face and then into Ben's. Then she flashed that quick smile again.

"Sorry—I was wrong to assume—it's just that, Jill, you said you had found my name in the records of the public meetings, and then there was all the coverage in the local paper. . . . But . . . again, I'm sorry. I'm used to dealing with other lawyers, and reporters, too."

She took a deep breath. "I had to stop being the attorney for the Historical Society because my maiden name is Oakes—I'm one of the captain's direct descendants."

"Oh," Ben said.

A second later, Jill said it again—"Oh!"

Because that meant she was part of the group that had sold its property rights. This woman had been paid half a million dollars by the town of Edgeport.

Mrs. Burgess looked back and forth between them as she talked. "I was against the Glennley plan back then, and I still am. But the town offered the heirs money in exchange for all future claims against the property, and a number of my relatives really needed that cash. And I can't blame them—five hundred thousand dollars is a lot of money for most people. I mean, it's a lot for me, too, but I've had a good career for a long time, and so has my husband. I didn't need that money the way some of my relatives did. So I went along with the group of heirs—it was that, or have my own family mad at me forever." She looked out the window. "It was an ugly situation."

She paused again, looking past Ben into the sky behind him. "But do I still wish there had been some way to stop the deal? You bet I do. I'm not some preservation nut who wants to lock Edgeport into the past, but the kind of changes this theme park is going to bring? I just don't think the town council members did their homework on this deal—or else they all stand to make a *lot* of money from it. Either way, it's bad—and either way, it's too late now."

Ben tensed up. He looked over at Jill, and she was looking at him, one eyebrow lifted. Was this someone they could trust?

Ben turned back to Mrs. Burgess. "I've got another legal question. If a kid tells something to a lawyer, does the lawyer have to keep that confidential?"

Mrs. Burgess smiled. She seemed glad to talk about something less personal. "Well, that depends. If the state appointed me to defend the rights of a young person accused of a crime, then yes, everything we talked about would be held in strict confidence. Or if parents hired me to protect the rights of their child? Same thing—full confidentiality."

Jill rustled around in her backpack, and Ben

thought she was looking for a pencil. But she pulled out a dollar bill, reached across the table, and handed it to Mrs. Burgess. The lawyer looked puzzled, but she smiled a little.

Jill smiled back and said, "Okay, let's say a kid just walks into your office and hands you a dollar, and says, 'Here, I want to hire you and ask you some legal questions.' And then you talked. Would *you* have to keep everything the kid talked about a secret?"

The lawyer's smile vanished. Her eyes narrowed, and she looked from Jill to Ben, and then back to Jill again. With a voice that sounded hard and flat, she said, "Tell me what all this is really about. Right now."

Ben leaned forward in his chair as Jill and the lawyer faced each other, eye to eye. And Jill didn't blink. She was magnificent.

"First," Jill said, "answer my question."

In the same tough voice, Mrs. Burgess said, "All right. I'm going to talk like a lawyer now, so stop me if you don't understand. I am an active member of the Massachusetts bar, which means I am authorized by this state to try civil and criminal cases in open court. Therefore, I am also considered an officer of the court. I am also a law-abiding citizen of the

Commonwealth. As a citizen or as a lawyer, if I learn that some crime has been committed, I am legally bound to report it to the proper authorities—and I would. But if a person is my *client*, then there is a circumstance called attorney-client privilege. This means I have to keep whatever my client says a secret. So that's the *general* rule about confidentiality. With me so far?"

Ben had a question, but he kept quiet and nodded. So did Jill.

"Now," the lawyer said, looking Jill in the eye, "you have outlined a *particular* situation to me. So now I shall speak in specifics. A minor, a person under the age of eighteen, comes to my office and offers me payment for a service—my legal advice. Therefore, this *specific* situation means that a minor and a lawyer are entering into a formal agreement—which is called a contract. In Massachusetts, and in most other states, no one under the age of eighteen can enter into a *legally binding* contract. Therefore, *legally* speaking, the short answer to your question is *no*—no, you cannot hire me as your lawyer, because you are too young to enter into a legally binding contract. And since you cannot make a contract and become my client, the rules of attorney-client privilege or confidentiality would not apply. *Legally*. Understand?"

Jill nodded, trying to keep her face neutral. But Ben could see the disappointment.

"*However*," the lawyer said, raising one finger, "I have one more very important point to make: As long as I do not learn of any crime that has been committed, then I would consider myself *ethically* bound to keep whatever was said to me in the strictest confidence forever—because that would be the *right* thing to do. And in my own practice as an attorney, doing what is *ethically right* is at least as important as doing what is *legally* correct."

She handed the dollar back to Jill. "So . . . remembering what I've just said about criminal activity, why don't you tell me what's on your mind?"

Again, Ben and Jill looked at each other. Jill nodded first, and Ben nodded back.

He reached into his backpack, pulled out a single piece of paper, and slid it across the low table to Mrs. Burgess.

She took a pair of reading glasses from the pocket of her jacket. She perched them on her nose and picked up the paper.

Ben watched her eyes. Starting at the top of the sheet, they scanned from side to side like the needle on a lie detector. And her eyes opened wider and wider as she got to the bottom of the page. She repeated the whole process, and by the end of the second scan, her eyes were still wide open—and so was her mouth.

"Where did you get this?" she gasped. Then, "No, wait, don't answer—I don't want to know that. Here's a safer question: Is it your hope that this document could be used to keep the Oakes School from being torn down?"

Ben and Jill both nodded.

"Well, then I have bad news." She tapped the sheet of paper. "This remarkable little piece of history is called a codicil—a new provision that is being *added* to a will. In order for a codicil to have any power at all, the will that it's being added to must also be in force. And the captain's will, at least the part related to the school and its property, is as good as dead. The heirs gave up their rights under that will by accepting payments from the town, and the town has accepted partial payment from the Glennley Group. Full and final title to the school property will pass from the town of Edgeport to the Glennley Group the day after school's out in June—which is how far away?"

"Twenty-one days," said Jill. Ben smiled slightly—it was just like Jill to have the timeline all worked out.

"Which means," the lawyer went on, "that in three weeks, the captain's will *and* this codicil will both become completely meaningless—dead."

That last word hung in the air for about five seconds.

Then Ben said, "But if the whole deal isn't completely settled, couldn't we take the actual codicil to a judge tomorrow? Wouldn't that work?"

Mrs. Burgess nodded. "It might—but if you take this to the Essex County Probate Court over in Salem tomorrow, by Monday morning a squad of Glennley's lawyers are going to be all over it. Motions, counter-filings, allegations of foul play—you name it. They will swarm and snap at this with every tooth they have. And don't forget the media—this would be a big news story, and it would be exploited. And the legal process of sorting everything out? That could take a long, long time."

"But wouldn't that still stop them from tearing down the school?" asked Jill.

"It might delay the demolition, at least for a while. But there are so many question marks, so many ways to attack this codicil—issues of authenticity, questions about the witness and the date, not to mention the fact that there's no individual named as the new inheritor here, only 'the bearer'—legally, it's a big mess."

The lawyer paused, looking at both of them. "Also, if you wanted to put this into play, I couldn't be involved. It's called conflict of interest. I have already benefited from the Glennley deal, and for me to turn around now and represent someone who opposes it? That would cause . . . complications. But if you choose to go ahead with this, I'll be very happy to give you the name of a good person who can help."

Again, Ben and Jill exchanged looks.

Ben said, "We need to think about it."

Mrs. Burgess stood up. She handed Ben the copy of the codicil. "That sounds like the wise thing to do."

They walked to the door of her office, and she shook Jill's hand.

"Thank you for your time," Jill said, "and for the advice."

"My pleasure," said Mrs. Burgess. "Meeting you two has been the nicest thing that's happened in this office for months. And I wish both of you all the best."

She turned to Ben, and as they shook hands he said, "Could I ask one more question?"

"Of course."

"If we *did* want to try to use the codicil, when do we have to get it to the courthouse in Salem?"

"That's an easy one," she said, all business again. "You've got *exactly* twenty-one days."

CHAPTER 12

For Real

After a night of tossing and turning, Ben woke up early Friday morning in a cold sweat. What if that original codicil had fallen out of the old book? And what if Lyman had found it, lying on the floor by the reference shelves, or maybe in the library workroom? Or what if Robert had looked through that book once more, spotted the codicil, and decided to feature it in his super report? And then there was also the chance that Ms. Shubert might have read it and taken to the principal right away . . . or to a lawyer.

As he lay there looking up through his window at the clouds, he imagined one nightmare scenario after another.

But the thought of Lyman discovering the codicil? *That* was the fear that yanked Ben up and out of bed. He was showered, dressed, and downstairs at quarter of seven.

His mom was already sitting at the kitchen table in her robe and slippers, both hands wrapped around a mug of tea, the local paper spread out in front of her.

"My goodness!" She glanced at the clock. "I must be dreaming!"

Ben smiled. "I've got to go to the library before school."

"This early?"

He nodded. "For that history project. There's a reference book I need—I can't check it out."

"Well," she said, "sit down and have a bite of breakfast."

"Can't—I have to be there when the doors open."

He took a banana from the counter and a granola bar from the pantry and slipped them into the pocket of his jacket. On his way past the table he leaned over and got a kiss on the cheek.

"Have a good day, sweetheart."

"I will, Mom. You too."

He walked into the front hall and stopped to pat Nelson.

"And don't forget, we've got that movie tonight."

"Right, *The Sea Hawk*—can't wait!"

He pulled the front door open.

"Call me if you'll be late, all right?"

"I will."

He pushed the storm door wide.

"And watch the traffic on Central Street."

"I always do. Bye."

He pulled the front door shut, and as the storm door wheezed, his mom called, "Bye-bye!"

Sheesh! Had she always been like that? Or was it worse in the past few months, since Dad went to live on the boat?

Hard to say. As he pulled back the peel and took two big bites of banana, he told himself that it didn't matter.

He had only taken about ten steps along the sidewalk when he began picturing the school library in his mind. He located his target, that large book—*A Man of the Sea, A School for the Ages*, which he thought was a great title. He knew right where it was kept.

First he'd have to find the document, fastened

in the back of the book . . . hopefully. Then he'd have to remove it from the book. Without damaging it. Without damaging the book, either. Then get it into his backpack . . . carefully. He'd have to keep it safe the whole day—where could he put it during sixth-period gym? When he got it home after school, then he'd need to hide it somewhere completely secure. Like up in his room behind his dresser—somewhere Nelson wouldn't be able to sniff it out and chew it to bits.

It was a lot to do. No point in worrying, though—until he got to school. Which meant he had about six minutes. But the fear made him pick up his pace. He took one last bite of banana, stuffed the peel back into his jacket pocket, and broke into a quick jog.

Ben switched his eyes and feet onto autopilot and tried to think about nothing in particular.

Movie night coming up—*The Sea Hawk*. He remembered watching it with his folks for the first time back when he was seven. Lots of action, huge ships, big battle scenes with cannon fire and swordplay, and sailors swinging on ropes above the burning decks.

The hero in the movie . . . Captain Thorpe . . . hmm. Was he based on someone from real life? And . . . if Thorpe *was* a real-life sea captain, could Captain Oakes have met him, met the *real* Sea Hawk? He'd have to check the dates—but then Ben remembered a scene where Captain Thorpe met with Elizabeth the First, Queen of England. So a meeting of the two captains would have been impossible. Elizabeth was queen *way* before the American Revolution. Way before Duncan Oakes was even born.

Amanda Oakes.

Amanda Oakes Burgess. The lawyer.

When she'd told that about herself? Amazing. And what she had said about the money the town had offered her and her relatives? Ben couldn't imagine how rich that lady was, not if she had actually wanted to turn down the five hundred thousand dollars they were offering . . . would *he* have done that? If someone said, *Here, Ben, here's half a million bucks right now, today, and all you have to do is forget this Keepers of the School stuff, just forget about it and walk away*—what would he do? Ben felt pretty sure he'd say, *No way! Pretty* sure . . .

As they'd walked to Jill's building after yesterday's meeting, both of them had been quiet, thinking about what the lawyer had advised.

Then, at her doorway, Jill had said, "If we use that codicil, everything about the Keepers will have to come out into the open, right? So . . . I think it should only be used as a last resort."

He had agreed with that, but then they'd had an argument about how long to wait before going public. Jill finally accepted his timeline: They would hold off using the codicil until Tuesday, June 16—the last day of school. They also decided to start figuring out the next clues right away, and he'd been glad to see her get excited about searching for the other safeguards.

As he trotted across School Street, he smiled. That argument about the codicil had felt good to him—it was like the old Jill was back in action.

Still . . . he couldn't shake the feeling that she was worried about something else, something big. The weird moods, that outburst on Wednesday—and then yanking out all those surveying stakes? That was just plain crazy.

Yeah, she seemed better, but there was trouble

brewing. It felt like a storm that was twenty miles off the coast—no damage yet, but the waters were churned up, and something bad might hit any moment, a real disaster.

But he couldn't think about Jill anymore, not now.

Ben had never arrived at school this early before. There were only six cars out back in the faculty parking lot. Even the "Reserved for Principal" slot was empty, the nurse's, too.

Best of all, he didn't see Lyman's truck anywhere. It was usually backed into the loading dock beside the janitor's workroom. On Monday after the funeral he had gotten a good look at it, parked on Union Street. It was a big Ford pickup, dark gray. It had red leather seats with wood grain finish around the dashboard. Double hub rear wheels too—two tires on each side. Nice truck. Expensive—a truck that might be hard to afford on a custodian's salary.

Lyman probably used it to haul his sailboat around.

Ben hurried past the loading dock and went around to the front of the building. The main door wasn't open this early, so he pushed the button to ring the office. He waved to Mrs. Hendon through the glass and held up his yellow hall pass. She gave him a cheery wave and buzzed him in.

Mrs. Sinclair smiled when he came into the library, and he headed right for the reserved books. The reference area wasn't very far from the front desk, but Ben had already worked out a plan. He set his book bag on the table closest to the reference shelf. Then he took off his jacket and laid it on top of his book bag.

The book he needed was right there, just three feet away.

It was good Ms. Shubert hadn't come in yet. She might have paid closer attention to Ben. She might have noticed him pulling that book off the shelf—the one she had recently repaired.

He set the heavy volume on the table in just the right spot. If Mrs. Sinclair happened to glance his way, the book would be hidden behind a large orange backpack and a blue windbreaker.

Ben turned the book over and opened the back cover. Beginning at the very last page, he worked fast, flipping first through the index, then page after page of footnotes. After that came a short note about the author, and finally—a page that up until two days ago had been completely blank.

Ms. Shubert had done a fine job taping the codicil exactly in the center of the large page, but Ben didn't have time to admire her work.

He took a quick look at the front desk. Mrs. Sinclair was busy at the keyboard, eyes locked on her screen.

He pulled out his small steel ruler and slipped the edge under one corner of the document, then pried gently upward. He did the same thing at each of the other three corners, and just like that, the codicil came free. There was still some tape on each corner, but there'd be plenty of time to deal with that later.

He closed the book and set the document face-down on the table. He quickly pulled his notebook out of his backpack and flipped it open to a pocket divider. He slipped the codicil gently between the flaps and closed his notebook.

Then, looking toward the front desk once more, he slid the book back onto the shelf and sat down.

Done! The whole process had taken only a minute and a half.

He leaned back and took some deep breaths, trying to get his heart to slow down. After about thirty seconds, it did. This was going to be a good day—an excellent day. Now he could actually relax a little.

Except . . . since he had some extra time before homeroom? He should double-check the dates and titles on his sketch of the Jack London time line. As he thought that, he was struck with a horrible idea—*I'm turning into Robert!*

He found his language arts folder anyway and pulled out the time line. No way would he ever become a Robert—he just wanted a good grade. Like Robert . . . hmm.

He quickly forgot about all that as he gathered his pile of notes and articles. It took him awhile to get it all organized—but he knew he had to because Robert was sure to inspect his research materials.

The first on the literary time line was a story called "Typhoon off the Coast of Japan," published when Jack London was only seventeen. Great title— probably a great story, too.

He had read *The Call of the Wild*, and he'd loved it. But this time line had made him realize how many sea stories the man had written—and he had never read any of them. . . .

Ben looked at the clock—only seven forty-five. Tons of time.

He got up, walked to the fiction shelves, found the *L* authors, and pulled out a book called *Stories of Ships and the Sea*. He checked the table of contents—yes! The typhoon story was at the top of the list.

Ben hurried back to his table, opened the book to page seven, and dove in.

After six or seven paragraphs, he was sort of disappointed. The language was old-fashioned, and there didn't seem to be much plot. But the description was great, and the stuff about setting out in small boats to hunt for seals in foul weather was interesting, so he kept reading.

Then the typhoon struck, and belowdeck, one of the crew was dying. Ben was hooked now, totally into the story, leaning forward over the book.

> Quite a sea was rolling by this time,
> occasionally breaking over the decks,
> flooding them and threatening to smash
> the boats. At six bells we were ordered
> to turn them over and put on storm
> lashings. This occupied us till eight bells,

when we were relieved by the mid-watch.
I was the last to go below, doing so just as
the watch on deck . . .

"Hey—I was hoping you'd be here."

Ben hated to leave the raging storm, but he blinked himself back to the library. It was Jill, and she sat down beside him. "Good book?"

"Yeah, Jack London. For that report I'm doing with Robert." He closed the book and slid it to one side. If she saw he was reading ocean adventure stories, she'd probably make some wisecrack about him being the sailor boy.

She glanced around, then whispered, "Did you check on the codicil?"

Ben nodded. "Didn't just check on it—I took it back." He patted his notebook. "I got really worried about it last night. Safer to keep it hidden at my house, don't you think?"

"Absolutely—that's good," she said.

Jill was still a moment. She put her hands on the table and looked at them, then picked a little at the edges of the Band-Aid on her right palm. "I . . . I wanted to ask you something. Don't take this the

wrong way, but do you think we might be making a big mistake here? Because stopping the theme park is also stopping the new middle school, and . . . the whole town *voted* on what it wanted. So it's like we're trying to turn everything around, all by ourselves. And all that stuff Mrs. Burgess said about the media? I mean, if we tried to use the codicil, could you deal with that, all the arguing, and tons of people in town hating you? I don't think . . . I mean, the town *voted*.

And the majority said, 'Yes, we want to trade an old school for something new.' And I just . . . I just want you to tell me how to think about it. Because I don't know anymore."

Ben stared at her, his jaw clenched so tight it felt he was going to pop the caps off his front teeth. But he wasn't angry. And he didn't know what to say.

"Um . . . I guess . . . I mean, I'm just . . . surprised by your question," he stammered. "Because, it's not like the *kids* in Edgeport got to vote about anything. And I thought . . . I thought we both thought it made sense, how someone needed to stand up for what Captain Oakes wanted to do, for *his* plan. He wanted kids to have a great school, right next to the ocean. And he knew that someday, somebody was going to think all this beautiful land was being wasted. On a school."

Ben paused. Jill was still looking at her hands.

"I can't tell you what to do, or how to think about this stuff. But it feels to me like the Glennley people didn't play fair, waving all their money in front of everybody. And from what we've found out about the captain, it seems like he was a really good person. I think *his* plan for this town is better than Glennley's plan. And all I know for sure is, if *I* don't try my best to keep the school safe, I'm gonna feel bad about that."

Jill turned to face him, but quickly shifted her eyes and looked past him. Her face went white.

Ben turned. It was Lyman, smiling down at them.

"Well, well, well . . . look who's here, right next to everybody's favorite reference book."

Ben didn't nod, didn't smile. He just looked the man in the eye. And gulped.

"I had quite a run-in with that assistant librarian back on Monday," Lyman said, still smiling. "She was upset with me for borrowing our special book all weekend—said that wasn't allowed, not even for staff. But I apologized, and all was forgiven. And I was sorry to hear that *you* almost got in trouble about that on Monday. . . ."

Ben kept the emotion off his face, but his heart was pounding.

Lyman had crept up from their left, and while he talked, he rolled the trash cart around the other side of the table until it blocked the aisle. Table in front of them, cart to their right, shelf behind them, and Lyman to their left. They were boxed in.

Lyman was still talking. "Then late yesterday

afternoon, outside in the parking lot? I saw Ms. Shubert, and I apologized again about causing a ruckus. And you know what? She got all friendly and chatty with me. And she told me how that book was *still* being a big problem, and how this picture had fallen out of it when *a couple of kids* were using it again the other day. And she thought it was so unusual, how that book had sat on the shelf for ten years, and suddenly everybody was looking at it. And she said she got some tape and put the picture back—made it all better. So I thought I'd stop in early this morning and take a look, make sure she did a good job. Because it's *such* a good book—here, would you mind passing it to me?"

Ben knew he had to move. But Jill was in his way—along with the big trash cart.

He stood up anyway, but instead of reaching for the old book, he quickly gathered up his notebook and folders and tucked everything into his backpack. He picked up the Jack London stories.

"Sorry," he said. "I've got to go check out this book."

Lyman's eyes narrowed, then he smiled slightly. "I don't think I'm going to find anything taped inside that old book, am I? Maybe you should hand me your backpack instead . . . how about that?"

Ben shook his head. He pressed his tongue against his front teeth. Fear numbed his mind. He felt like a mouse staring at a coiled snake, unable to move.

Lyman looked past him and smiled at Jill. She was still sitting, and she stared up at him, looking even more scared than Ben.

"I've got an interesting bit of news you two might like to know. Guess who just bought *two thousand shares* of preferred stock in a little company called Glennley Entertainment Group? Any clues? Some guy named Carl Acton—lives right here in Edgeport. Ever heard of him?"

Ben looked from Lyman's face to Jill's, then back again.

Lyman's smile got wider. "It looks like the young lady already knew about this, doesn't it? Seems like she's in a pickle. Does she keep working for some old dead janitor who imagined he could stop progress and keep this school from being torn down . . . or does she help her daddy get very, very rich? Hmm . . . what *will* she do?"

The smile vanished as he shifted his gaze and locked eyes with Ben.

"Listen to me carefully, Benjamin Pratt." His voice was low and harsh. "I don't know what kind of crazy ideas Mr. Keane put into your head, and I don't know what game you and your little friend Jill are playing, but it's time for all of it to stop. *Now*. Do you understand?"

Staring up into Lyman's face, Ben tried to remember how to look a tiger in the eye. He couldn't do it. The fear paralyzed him.

He felt a movement to his right. Jill was on her feet.

"Mr. Lyman, thank you so much for your entertaining performance. But Ben and I aren't afraid of you. We're just *not*. You're tall, and you're unpleasant to look at, and you know how to make your voice sound all deep and creepy, but you are a *fake*—a fake janitor who doesn't belong here. This is our *real* school. We are not fakes. Ben and I *belong* here. This is *our* school and *our* town, and this is the *real* beginning of our *real* school day." She paused, frowning up at Lyman a moment. Then she said, "I have no idea how you learned about my father's private business,

166

but I bet it isn't legal for you to know that. And whatever Ben or I do or *don't* do has *nothing* to do with you, at all. And now, you'll have to excuse us, because Ben and I are leaving for homeroom. In *our* school."

Ben was stunned, but he managed to nod and say, "Yeah, we're leaving."

Lyman glared at Jill, furious, his lips pressed together. Then he slowly shook his head. "You're not going anywhere till we're done with our talk."

"Oh yeah?" said Jill. "Watch."

Turning away from Lyman, she drew her right leg back, and then drove her knee forward with all her might and slammed it into the plastic barrel on the trash cart. The cart jumped two feet as a huge *boom* filled the library, and at that same instant, Jill yelled, "*OW!*"

Mrs. Sinclair's head jerked sideways, and she jumped up and trotted to the reference area.

"Jill! What happened? Are you all right?"

"That stupid trash cart, it was right in the way, and I banged my knee into it. . . . *Owww*."

Mrs. Sinclair frowned at the trash cart, and then at Lyman. "You can't block the aisles, not when students are here."

Jill began limping toward the front desk, and Mrs. Sinclair held her right elbow. Ben followed close behind.

"Let's go have the nurse look at that."

Jill lifted her right foot high as they neared the desk, flexing her knee, and she seemed to limp less with each step. She was making a speedy recovery. "Thanks, but I think it's okay—hardly hurts at all now."

Ben had to hide a grin.

"Well," said Mrs. Sinclair, "if it bothers you later, especially going up or down the stairs, you go straight to the nurse's office, all right?"

"I will," she said.

Ben put the Jack London book on the desk. His heart was beating so fast it was difficult to speak. "I need to check this out, please."

"Of course."

She opened the front cover and scanned the bar code, then slipped a date card into the pocket and handed Ben the book.

"Thanks, Mrs. Sinclair."

"You're welcome, Ben. And Jill, I'm so sorry you bumped your knee."

"It's okay," she said. "I'll be fine."

They went out the door and turned left toward the office.

Ben almost started jumping up and down. He spun all the way around, then walked backward out in front of Jill, grinning at her. "Incredible!" he gasped. "*That* . . . was *the* most amazing . . . ! I—I don't know what to say! Really—Jill! That was . . . *amazing!*"

Jill just walked. She shook her head. "Stop being so goofy—calm down. And stop walking backward."

Ben fell in next to her, but he was still bouncing a little. "Really, though, that was really something, everything you said."

Jill didn't answer.

So Ben stopped talking and walked, trying to put it all together.

"So, that stuff about your dad . . . all that's true?"

Ben had met Jill's father. He was short and wide, a fast talker. He owned both of the Dunkin' Donuts shops in town, and was half owner of Parson's Marina too. A serious businessman.

"It's all true," Jill said. "Here I am, trying to stop

the Glennley deal, and my dad wants it to happen right now, big-time. And all those months when my mom was trying to stop the project, going to those hearings and everything? They argued about it all the time, both of them yelling and stomping around the house—it was awful. But then the town voted, and it was settled, and everything went back to normal. And now . . ." She shrugged.

She didn't have to finish.

Ben saw all the pieces drop into place. He knew why Jill had seemed so anxious all week. If she helped him, and somehow they were able to stop the new amusement park, her parents might start fighting again. And her dad would lose money, which would make things worse. And maybe her dad would get mad at her for being involved, and then her mom might get mad at her dad for being mad at Jill . . . on and on. Then, what if her parents split up because of this, because of her? Seeing Ben over the past couple of months, living one week with his mom and the next week with his dad? Jill didn't want a mess like that in *her* family. And Ben didn't blame her, not one bit. She had every right to feel upset!

But . . . then what just happened in the library?

"So," Ben said cautiously, "what made you say all that just now?"

"Lyman. When he said that about my dad. My dad's good at what he does, and he's honest and he works hard, and buying that Glennley stock was a good move for him. Nothing wrong with it at all. But Lyman was using that, trying to keep me from doing something that *I* know is right. And I got mad."

"And sarcastic," said Ben, grinning. "Dramatic, too. Fantastic! Seriously, I wish I had it all on video—talk about an instant YouTube classic: Giant Janitor Smackdown!"

Jill smiled, but she wasn't ready to laugh. Ben could see she was still working through what had happened, trying to understand it. And really, he was too.

As they passed the office, the first busloads of kids burst through the front doors behind them, and the hall filled with the sounds of tromping feet, laughing and yelling, lockers banging open and slamming shut, teachers trying to quiet things down and control traffic. The school day was off and running.

Jill looked down at the floor as they walked. "Everything I said to Lyman?" she said. "It's true . . .

just true. This is *our* school. And this is *our* time to be here, right now. And linking up with Captain Oakes and this whole Keepers thing? That's part of it. What you said to me? That's true too—the captain's plan *is* better. It just is. And I've got to follow through and do my part. Right now, no matter what. We both have to, even though we'll be going on to the junior high next year. We still have to do our best."

"That's right," Ben said. "We have to."

She looked over at him and smiled. For Ben, it was the best moment of the whole week.

Jill turned away, then nudged his arm. "Look, up ahead."

It was Lyman, about twenty feet away, pushing the trash cart toward the custodian's workroom. He hadn't noticed them yet, but they were on a collision course.

Ben hesitated. "Let's go back, go up the south stairs," he said. "No tiger teasing, remember?"

Jill kept walking. She shook her head. "Nope. The rules have changed."

Lyman saw them, and he stopped at his doorway, leaning forward on the gray container, his face expressionless as they approached.

Jill slowed down and smiled at him. She pointed at the trash bin. "I'm glad you're being careful with that, Mr. Lyman. Don't want anybody to get hurt."

Ben expected an explosion, but it didn't come.

Lyman scowled straight ahead, then muttered, "That was a cute trick back there."

"Cute?" Jill said softly. "No—it was inventive and imaginative. Using a phony business card and pretending to be a yacht broker when you snooped around Ben's boat last week? *That* was cute."

Lyman turned and looked at her a long moment, but again, Ben saw no expression in the man's eyes. Like a snake.

Then, angling his face away again, Lyman suddenly smiled. And when he spoke, his voice was low, but sharp and sardonic. "Well, whatever you're trying to do, you kids go ahead and have fun, all right? Knock yourselves out. Because in three weeks, there'll be *nothing* here—just a big hole filled in with rubble."

"We'll see about that," said Jill.

Then, with a fierce little smile, she said, "Come on, Ben. We've got *school* today."

Ben began walking away with Jill, when suddenly he turned and called, "Hey, Mr. Lyman, wait a second." The man stopped in the doorway of the janitor's workroom. Ben walked back, pulled the banana peel out of his jacket pocket, and dropped it into the trash barrel. Then he looked Lyman right in the eye, smiled, and said, "Thanks."

CHAPTER 13

Duped

Some kind of brilliant recklessness had definitely gotten into Jill on Friday morning, and some of it must have rubbed off on Ben. Because shortly after Jill's second run-in with Lyman, Ben was just about to walk into his homeroom . . . when he stopped.

A slightly crazy idea popped into his head, and he decided to go for it.

He walked right past the art room and ducked out a door onto the playground. He climbed up onto Captain Oakes's gravestone—and waited. He sat still as the warning bell rang, still waiting. It wasn't until after the final bell clanged that Ben climbed down and went into his homeroom.

He was late. On purpose.

Of course, Ms. Wilton immediately gave him a detention—which was exactly what he wanted.

All during the school day, no matter how many times Lyman came around a corner or popped through a doorway, no matter how many times the man seemed to be watching him and tracking his every move around the old building, Ben wasn't annoyed at all. And he was looking forward to staying after school.

When the ship's bell rang for dismissal, Ben found Jill at her locker, and they made plans to meet up at Parson's Marina on Saturday afternoon. And then he walked down the north stairwell and got to the art room at exactly 2:50, ready to serve his detention. But instead of sitting down at a table to read or do some homework, he walked to the front of the room.

"Hey, Ms. Wilton, anything I can do to help out?"

"Sure, that'd be great. Let's see—how about hanging up these fourth-grade paintings on that first wire by the wall? The clothespins are in that blue bin. You'll have to stand on a chair, so be careful. And some of the tempera is still wet."

Hanging the paintings took about ten minutes,

177

and then Ms. Wilton asked him to wipe down all the tables with a big sponge. As he worked, Ben kept an eye on the clock. If his plan was going to work, the timing had to be perfect.

With four minutes left on his detention, Ben went to work on the bucket of tempera brushes soaking in the big sink. He had to rinse out all the paint, shake off most of the water, smooth the bristles, and then lay each brush flat on a table covered with newspapers.

Ben adjusted the temperature of the water. He gave the hot faucet handle three turns, then did the same to the cold. Then he gave the cold handle four more turns. Then he cranked it some more until it was wide open. The water blasted into the bucket, kicking up a brown foam. Ben kept turning. He used both hands and turned that cold water handle with all his strength. Suddenly the handle spun around, free as a pinwheel, and the water gushed and gushed.

"Um, Ms. Wilton? Something happened to this faucet—I can't shut off the cold water."

"*Again?* Arrgh! I cannot *wait* to get my new art room!"

She glanced at the clock. "You can leave now,

Ben, but go find Mr. Lyman for me, all right? And tell him to hurry!"

"Sure," said Ben.

Out in the hallway, a flash of panic hit him. This was the part of his scheme that couldn't be planned. He needed to find a kid who would go and hunt for Lyman and tell him about the newest plumbing disaster in the art room.

The halls were almost empty—slim pickings. Then Ben grinned.

"Hey, Robert!"

Robert Gerritt was rushing from the Annex hallway into the old building, a book in one hand and a bag of potato chips in the other. He didn't slow down.

"Pratt—what are you doing here? No, let me guess: detention, right? Can't talk, got to go catch Hinman."

Ben fell in beside him, trotting to keep up. "Listen, Ms. Wilton needs Lyman in the art room right away—flooded sink. Can you find him and tell him to hurry? As a favor?"

Robert made a grimace. "You crazy? Find him yourself, Pratt. I've got stuff to do."

"I really need you to do this, Robert. Really, a

favor. And it'll make us even. You know, from when I saved your *life* and everything."

That stopped Robert, and he wheeled to face Ben, his eyes blazing. "That is *low*, Pratt, really low. But, you know what? I accept your terms: I go and find Lyman, and then I owe you *nothing*. Deal?"

Ben smiled and nodded. "Deal." He put out his hand, and they shook on it.

Robert took off down the hallway again, and outside the janitor's door he bellowed, "Mr. Lyman?" No answer. He was headed for the south stairwell, but when he reached the corner of the hallway, he looked toward the office and yelled again, "Mr. Lyman?"

There was a faint reply, and Robert rushed through the doorway of the south stairwell. Ben heard him call out, "Big flood, Mr. Lyman, down in the art room. Ms. Wilton wants you to hurry."

Ben smiled. Perfect—Lyman was on the second or third floor.

Ben went halfway down the hall and ducked into the boys' room across from the janitor's workshop. He slipped into the third stall by the wall, closed the door, and waited.

A minute or two later, he heard the keys jangling

from Lyman's belt, then heard the latch and opening door as he went into the workroom.

He could picture Lyman there at the bench, picking up parts, dropping tools into the canvas bag. Soon the workroom door wheezed open again, and he heard the clank of the big rolling bucket against the door frame.

From down the hallway Ms. Wilton called out, "Hurry, please, it's overflowing!"

Peeking out, he saw Lyman go into the art room, saw the door shut behind him. Ben opened the boys' room door wider, looking both ways. All clear.

Moving fast, he was out the door, across the hall, and inside the custodian's room, his heart racing, his palms sweating, his mouth dry as cornflakes. Because now he was going to try to keep that promise he had made to Tom Benton at Mr. Keane's funeral. If there was an old green tackle box somewhere in this workroom, he had about six minutes to find it, and then get the heck out of there.

But first, Ben trotted to the end of the room and checked the door that opened onto the loading dock. He tested the push bar and made sure it was working. That was his emergency exit.

Under the workbench—that's where Tom said he might have left his tackle box. Ben groaned as he scanned the bench. It had to be at least twenty feet long, and it was a colossal mess. Racks and bins and all kinds of tools cluttered the top surface, and the wide lower shelf was overflowing with a bewildering assortment of junk, stuff that had been thrown and dropped and stuffed down there year after year, decade after decade. Electric motors, boxes of rusty chain, coffee cans full of nuts and bolts, a crate of electrical fuses, boxes and bins of toilet parts, pipe, window latches, hinges, doorknobs, coils of wire— there was no end to it, and that was just the lower shelf itself. The floor *below* the shelf was also packed.

Ben shrugged off his backpack and took out his flashlight so he could see back into the shadows. He started at the left end of the bench, working quickly but carefully, scanning the shelf, then the floor below, moving anything that blocked his view, opening the lid of any box or bin large enough to hide a tackle box. His hands were dusty and grimy, and he kept having to brush the spiderwebs off his face and arms.

He worked silently, straining to hear the slightest jangle of Lyman's keys or the tiniest clank of that rolling bucket. His heart wouldn't stop pounding, and he kept flicking his tongue against his capped teeth.

After three minutes he was less than halfway along the length of the bench. He wasn't going to have enough time. Ben stood up and arched his back, thinking . . . and then he froze. Keys! And footsteps, coming fast.

He swooped to his left, grabbed his backpack, and kept going, straight for the wall where the big rolling trash cart was parked. He scooted behind it, dropped flat on the floor, clicked off his flashlight, and held his breath.

With one eye, Ben saw the bottom of the hallway door swing inward, and Lyman's big booted feet walked right to the workbench. He stood there, muttering. "Valve stems . . . valve stems . . . somewhere, somewhere . . . ," and Ben heard parts drawers pulled open and slammed shut, five or six of them in quick succession. Then, "There we go!" The feet turned around, took three long steps toward the doorway, and Lyman was gone.

Ben let out a long breath, but he lay still until he no longer heard the jangling keys or the heavy footsteps.

He stood up, feeling shaky but relieved. He also had new information—Lyman had to replace the faucet valve stem, which would have to take him at least another five minutes . . . probably.

Ben flipped on his light again and rushed back into the search, pawing through junk, pushing old paint cans out of the way, determined that if a pale green tackle box was actually there, he was going to find it.

Soon he had worked his way all the way to the right end of the bench. He stood up and turned off his flashlight. His knees hurt almost as much as his arms and neck. He was disappointed, but at least he'd be able to tell Tom Benton he'd made a real effort. Plus he had won a small secret victory over Lyman. Who knows, maybe Tom hadn't left the tackle box here at all, maybe it was tucked away down in the storage locker at . . .

Ben stopped midthought. At the far right edge of the bench, right up on top, something was sticking out from under a stack of blue shop rags. It was definitely a box—rounded edges, metal, and pale green with rust spots.

Ben pulled off the stack of rags, and there it was! Across the top of the tackle box, nearly worn away by time and hard use, a name had been painted in black letters with a small brush: Tommy Benton.

Ben grabbed it by the handle, and like Tom had said, it felt heavy, maybe five or ten pounds. He hurried over and retrieved his backpack from behind the trash bin, unzipped the biggest pouch, and stuffed the tackle box in—a tight fit, but he managed to get the zippers closed.

Ben made a quick detour to the big sink. Anybody he met would surely notice all the grime on his hands, and that might lead to questions.

As he dried his hands on a rag, he looked at the workbench to make sure it didn't look any different... nope. Still a gigantic mess. He slipped the backpack straps over his shoulders and turned toward the hallway door, then stopped. He trotted to the loading dock entrance. He opened the wide gray door enough to look around—no one nearby. A much safer exit than the hallway.

He stepped out onto the concrete platform, walked to the side, took the four steps down, went across the parking area to the path leading toward School Street, and that was it. Now he was just another kid headed home after school.

Ben started to run, a slow, easy stride. He was still wound up, and it felt good to burn off some of the nervous energy. The heavy box banging against his back felt awkward and uncomfortable, but he didn't care. He had just pulled off a completely successful raid, right under Lyman's nose! And if he hurried, maybe he could hop on his bike and take the box over to BayHaven right away . . . and hope Tom wasn't at another funeral. He couldn't wait to see his face.

Ben jogged across Central Street and then sprinted for home, covering the last half block at a dead run. He veered onto his front walk, took the porch steps three at a time, and pulled to a stop at the door. There was a sudden weight shift on his back, and he jerked to his right just in time to see the tackle box and his social studies book tumble onto the porch floor—all the bouncing around had forced the backpack zippers open. Nelson began barking at him from the backyard.

The tackle box wasn't damaged, but the lid had popped open halfway—no big deal. Ben stooped down and righted the box, then carefully picked up some rusty fishhooks and a red and white casting spool, and set them on the top tray. A bunch of the large weights

had tumbled out too, and he reached for them—then stopped cold. Amid the gray lead sinkers there were two coins, a bright gold one, and another that looked almost black.

He picked up the gold coin and stared at the face of a man with a sloping nose, plump cheeks, and long hair that looked kind of like a ponytail.

There were fancy designs stamped on the flip side, with writing around the edge in capital letters. Then he saw the date and almost dropped the thing—1775!

He picked up the other coin and recognized that one right away—a Massachusetts Pine Tree shilling. It was one of the first silver coins minted in the colonies, something he'd learned about just a month ago. It was tarnished and worn, but the date was clear—1652!

Two coins, both old, both of them certainly valuable—very cool! But . . . how come they were in Tom's tackle box? Had he left them there? Definitely something to ask him about.

Ben knew his mom wasn't home yet, but she

would be soon. He didn't want to have to explain any of this, so he quickly dropped everything into the box and began to close the lid—then flipped it open wide. And he stared.

The entire bottom of the tackle box was covered with gold coins, had to be forty or fifty of them, and more shillings, too!

Staring at all that gold and silver, Ben realized something instantly: Tom Benton had tricked him! All that stuff about how he wanted his old tackle box "just to have it"? Right . . . *nobody* could forget about treasure like this.

For some reason, Tom had left the box hidden at the school, and now he needed it back. So he'd recruited Ben to be his errand boy.

Ben latched the box, then picked it up along with his social studies book. Once inside, he went right to the kitchen and found a memo pad, ignoring Nelson's whining outside the back door.

Hi, Mom— got home about 3:15.
Riding over to BayHaven Care on
High Street, meeting with a retired
janitor—part of my extra credit
project. Home soon.
                    Love you, Ben

Less than two minutes later Ben was pedaling south on Central Street. The tackle box was wrapped in a brown paper sack, secured to the rack above his rear wheel with three bungee cords—there weren't going to be any spills during this trip. He had to get the box over to BayHaven in one piece, and hand it to Tom Benton himself.

And then ask him a couple of questions.

CHAPTER 14

Wages

High Street deserved its name. As Ben banked his bike left off of Central, he had to squeeze both brake handles all the way down the block to the BayHaven Care building. The place had been a hotel back in the 1870s, a three-story gem with tall windows, round turrets, and a wide porch with rocking chairs for the summer visitors. It had always reminded Ben of a castle. The rockers were still there, and half a dozen were being used by some of the current residents.

He locked his bike to a handrail by the front steps, and before unwrapping the bungee cords from the tackle box, he looked out across the bay.

The water was silver and shiny blue all the way to the horizon. Tom Benton had told him that this place had a good view of the water, and he'd been right. Ben could have stood there until sunset. But he had business inside.

A young woman with dark hair and a nice smile looked up at him from behind a counter in the foyer. She wasn't dressed like a nurse, and the place didn't smell like nurses worked there. It smelled more like the library at school.

"Hello, may I help you?"

"Yes, thanks. I'd like to see Tom Benton."

One eyebrow went up a little, and her smile got a little brighter. "Is he expecting you?"

"No, I just stopped by. And I brought him something."

The woman rose up slightly in her chair and looked at the package under Ben's arm.

"You're not bringing him groceries, are you? Like steaks, or a roasting chicken? Because we have a rule about cooking in the guest rooms, and Tom—Mr. Benton—he has trouble obeying that rule."

"No, there's no food. It's just . . . a storage container, a box." Ben said that because there might also be a rule about having big rusty fishhooks around the place.

"Good. Now . . . ," she said, looking down at a log book, "I know that he's here this afternoon, and he lives in suite 207. You can go ahead up there, and I'll give him a quick ring to let him know you're coming. Your name, please?"

"Benjamin Pratt—and if he doesn't remember my name, say that I'm the kid who got some fruit for him on Monday, okay?"

"Will do. Have a nice visit, and you can use the elevator right behind me, there on the left."

"Thanks," said Ben.

The elevator was slow and creaky, loaded with dark walnut woodwork and brass grillwork, beautiful stuff. But by the time the door crept open at the second floor, Ben decided that as much as he loved old stuff, all elevators should be brand-new.

"Hey there, Benjamin Pratt, walk right this way!"

Tom Benton was standing in the doorway of his apartment, one hand gripping his walker, and waving with the other like Ben was a long-lost son.

Ben waved back. "Hey, Tom—it's great to see you."

When he reached the door, Tom shook his hand, and then kept hold of it, pulling him inside. "What a good surprise, you showing up like this. Come on over and sit awhile."

Tom's living room was bright and clean and uncluttered, not at all the way Ben had imagined a retired janitor's home would look. A pale gray slip-covered couch sat against one wall, and next to the windows a pair of worn green velvet armchairs faced each other across a low table made of light-colored pine. The floor was polished hardwood, with one blue woven rug in front of the couch, and another larger one beneath the easy chairs and table. Tom quickly navigated his walker to the chair on the right and eased himself into it.

Ben looked out the window before he sat down. "I thought the view from the front porch was good, but this is amazing. What a great place!"

"Thank you very much," said Tom. "I like it here, I like it a lot." He nodded at the parcel under Ben's arm. "I'm thinking you've got a bowl of ripe strawberries and a quart of vanilla ice cream in there—am I right?"

"No," Ben said, "but I think you're going to like it anyway."

"So . . . it's a chocolate Bundt cake?"

"Nope," said Ben, laughing. "It's your old tackle box—I found it in the janitor's workroom, almost right where you said it would be."

Ben was looking at his face, watching for his reaction.

All he saw was delight—pure delight. Tom's eyes opened wide.

"Really? You found it? Let me see, let me see!"

Ben pulled the box out of the paper bag, and the old man's face lit up like a carnival ride.

Ben held on to the box, didn't make a move to hand it over. Still watching Tom's face, he said, "I have to tell you the truth—I dropped it on my front porch, and the lid opened up. And some things fell out . . . I'm sorry about that."

The smile left Tom's face and he looked at Ben for a long moment.

Without a word, he grabbed for his walker and pulled himself to his feet. Turning quickly, he shuffled toward the little galley kitchen. Ben could see a tiny microwave on the counter and a small refrigerator against the wall—no oven.

But Tom wasn't thinking about refreshments,

wasn't really going to the kitchen at all. He stopped next to a small arched pass-through, where a portable telephone and an answering machine sat on the shelf.

Tom said, "I want you to hear this," then punched a button on the call recorder.

There was a click, then a pause. "Tom? It's me. I want you to get your old tackle box. You know where it is. I left something for you. Can't talk now. Call me at home tomorrow."

Ben shivered, and the hairs on his arms stood up. It was Mr. Keane talking—a voice from the grave.

Leaning forward, Ben set the tackle box on the low table. He jumped as the machine made a loud beep.

A mechanical voice announced, "May 21 . . . ten thirty-three . . . a.m."

Tom spoke softly. "Want to listen again?"

Ben shook his head, and Tom moved back to his chair and sat down.

"So . . . that's what Roger told me. And about an hour later, he died. You can see why I wanted to know why he told me to fetch that box . . . but I knew I couldn't just waltz into the school and haul it away, even though my name's painted right on it. And after what you told me about Roger and that new janitor, well, that cinched it. So . . . I kinda set you up to go and get it for me. But I guess you've already figured that out." Tom paused and nodded at the tackle box. "And right now, you know more than I do, because I have no idea in the world what's in there."

Ben picked up the shopping bag and ripped it along one edge, then flattened it out on the table. Opening the tackle box, he turned it upside down onto the brown paper. Out tumbled all the hooks, the lead weights, the plastic bobbers, the lures, some tangled nylon line, a handful of rust flakes, and a large mound of gold and silver coins.

"Holy moly!" whispered Tom. "Gold?"

"Coins," Ben said, "and the dark ones are silver. I only looked at one of each. The gold one was dated 1775, and the silver one was a Pine Tree shilling from 1652. Pretty amazing, huh?"

"Hoo-*wee*, I should say! Must be a small fortune

there, the kinda stuff a coin collector would kill for! But . . . where did Roger get all that?"

Ben shrugged. "At school somewhere, that's what I decided when I was riding over here—except I thought it was you who'd found them. But after what Mr. Keane said, I think he must have found the coins hidden at school. I mean, he wouldn't have found them somewhere else and then taken them to the workroom—that makes no sense at all. Plus, the building's really old, and we know Captain Oakes was *definitely* into hiding stuff. So Mr. Keane found these, and he wanted to get them away from the school. When he called you he was already at the hospital, and he knew he was probably going to be away on sick leave. So he wanted your help. Probably wanted to share those coins with you. Sounded like you two were close friends."

Tom nodded slowly. "We really were. But I can't keep these—I mean, they're not mine. And they weren't Roger's, either. We've got to give these coins back."

"Um . . . ," Ben said, trying to think calmly, "I don't think that's a good idea, especially now. It would really get things stirred up." Ben knew it would do more than that. Every kid, every teacher, every single person at Captain Oakes School would get gold fever—they'd tear the building apart, looking for treasure. And people in the town? They'd come to the school grounds in the middle of the night with picks and shovels, digging for buried loot.

"I really think it's okay for you to keep the coins—I mean, who would we even give them to— Captain Oakes?"

Tom Benton didn't smile. He shook his head. "I can't keep what isn't mine—I just can't."

Thinking fast, Ben said, "But really . . . if this money was at the school, and Captain Oakes left it there where a janitor would find it . . . then it was like he was planning to pay you for all the years you worked for him. And he would have wanted to pay Mr. Keane, too."

"What're you talking about? We worked for the Edgeport Board of Education."

Ben reached into the front pocket of his cargo pants and pulled out the big gold coin. He held it up. "You carried this thing a long time, right?"

"Sure did, twenty-four years."

"And who was the janitor before you?"

"Jimmy Conklin."

"And when Jimmy gave you this token, did you promise to follow Captain Oakes's orders—didn't you promise you would defend his school for the children of Edgeport?"

Tom lunged forward in his chair and pulled himself to his feet, the knuckles of both his hands bright white as he gripped his walker. He glared down at Ben, eyes bright and fierce. "Absolutely! Jimmy made me swear on my sacred honor."

Ben was breathing fast now, and what to say next poured into his mind like a flood tide.

"Well, all those years you carried this, Captain Oakes *was* your boss, and you worked for *him*!" Ben recalled what Amanda Burgess had said to Jill, and added, "In fact, you and the captain had a *contract*, and for *twenty-four years* you held up your end of the deal, every single day. You were the Keeper of the School. And if Captain Oakes were right here, right now, you know what he'd do?" Ben dug his hand into the pile of coins and held up a fistful. "The captain would take all this money, and he'd stuff it into *your* pockets, and he'd say, 'Tom Benton, I am so *proud* of you, and this? This is your wages, and I want to thank you for the fine work you did for me and for all the children at my school—I thank you!'"

Tears welled up in the old man's eyes. He slowly settled back into his chair and turned to look out at the water. He was quiet, and Ben barely dared to breathe.

Still looking out to sea, Tom said, "It's a nice view here, but it's nowhere near as nice as the one from the school. The old captain knew what he was doing, don't you think?"

"Yes, I do," said Ben, dropping the handful of coins back onto the pile. "I think Captain Oakes knew *exactly* what he was doing. All we have to do is figure out what that was—and we have to do it soon."

Tom turned his head and looked at Ben. "Well, we're under attack, that's for darn sure, and my oath's still good. So count me in. Anything I can do, day or night, you call me. And for now, I'll hang on to the captain's money, and we'll see if there's a way we can use it. How about you count it all up so we've got a solid record."

Ben shook his head. "You said you'll keep it, and

that's all I need to know." He stood up, and so did Tom. Ben reached across the table, and they shook hands.

Ben smiled and said, "So, how does it feel to be defending the school again?"

Tom grinned. "It feels like that's what I've been doing my whole life."

"Me too," said Ben. "Me too."